the Boys of San Joaquin

Also by D. James Smith

Fast Company

*Probably the World's Best Story About a Dog
and the Girl Who Loved Me*

the Boys of San Joaquin

A NOVEL

BY D. JAMES SMITH

ALADDIN PAPERBACKS

New York   London   Toronto   Sydney

ALADDIN PAPERBACKS
An imprint of Simon & Schuster Children's Publishing Division
1230 Avenue of the Americas, New York, NY 10020
Text copyright © 2005 by D. James Smith
All rights reserved, including the right of reproduction in whole
or in part in any form.
ALADDIN PAPERBACKS and colophon are trademarks of
Simon & Schuster, Inc.
Also available in Atheneum Books for Young Readers hardcover edition.
Designed by Ann Zeak
The text of this book was set in Baskerville.
Manufactured in the United States of America
First Aladdin Paperbacks edition June 2006
2 4 6 8 10 9 7 5 3 1
The Library of Congress has cataloged the hardcover edition as follows:
Smith, D. J., 1955-
The boys of San Joaquin / D. James Smith.
p. cm.
"A Richard Jackson Book."
Summary: In a small California town in 1951, twelve-year-old Paolo and his deaf cousin Billy get caught up in a search for money missing from the church collection, leading them to complicated discoveries about themselves, other family members, and the townspeople they thought they knew.
[1. Coming of age—Fiction. 2. Family life—California—Fiction. 3. Theft—Fiction. 4. Italian Americans—Fiction. 5. Deaf—Fiction. 6. People with disabilities—Fiction. 7. California—History—1950—Fiction.] I. Title.
PZ7.S64464Bo 2005
[Fic]—dc22 2004003075
ISBN-13: 978-0-689-87606-6 (hc.)
ISBN-10: 0-689-87606-8 (hc.)
ISBN-13: 978-1-4169-1619-2 (pbk.)
ISBN-10: 1-4169-1619-9 (pbk.)

FOR MOM AND DAD
with love and wonder

Dad—a quiet one, came from Appalachia, old enough to have ten kids

Mother—a genuine Italian lady, never takes sass, probably my dad's age

Paolo—me, good-looking guy, smart, nice, twelve years old

Georgie—my little brother, still a kid, only six

Billy—my cousin, he's deaf but a smart one for being nine years old

Hector—my older brother, sort of shy, probably reads too much, eighteen years old

Ernie—oldest brother, a real storyteller, works full time, old enough to drink Hamm's beer, twenty-one

Margarita—my sister, pretty for a girl, sixteen years old, likes Jimmy Assayian

Shawna—sister, thirteen years old, another big reader

Betsy—sister, seventeen years old, more Appalachian than not

Aurora and Alice-Ann—more sisters, twins, ten years old, think it's funny to be disrespectful of older brothers

Maria-Teresina-the-Little-Rose—baby sister, four years old and bound to be trouble soon enough

Grandpa Leonardo—born in Italy, has a grocery store, about the age of most grandpas

Grandma Leonardo—very sweet and quiet, likes to let Grandpa think he's the boss, Grandpa's age

Uncle Charlie—my dad's brother, ex–coal miner from West Virginia, once a soldier, older than my dad

Rufus—my dog, three and a half years old, good nose, flunked dog-obedience school

Buster—girl milk goat, two years old, eats anything

Monsignor—an Irish person who is old enough to have white hair if he had any

Early—caretaker at the church, said to have relations in the Rockies he won't claim, probably sleeps a lot in winter

Terence—a strange one that I have got to know, age thirteen

Mr. Gaston—Terence's dad, probably forty years old, the only expert dancer in Orange Grove City

Theresa—girl my age who thinks she's interesting to boys, which she is not

CHAPTER 1

Now, THIS IS A STORY AS TRUE AS I KNOW HOW
to tell it. There are those that would say it's not
true, then, but they'd be wrong. I have a reputation
for stretching things toward the interesting, but only
as to make my point, so you'll understand that if this
isn't exactly the whole truth, it *is* as close as you want
it to be.

I was raised by an Old Testament father. The
kind who could burn holes in you just by looking if
he cared to. Had one big eye that lit up when he was
mad, eye as big as a mule's, stood out strong against
his other eye, sort of a sleepy burro's eye—a little

burro brother to that other one. Now, my dad and his good eye burned all lying from me by the time I was seven.

He's dead twenty years now, and I still feel him looking over my shoulder and watching I get things right. It's not like his mule eye is following me; it's more like I've got this black barn cat curled on my shoulder ready to swipe down, with claws out, to draw blood on these fingers if I stray from the truth.

I came up in a little town and a big family. Six sisters and three brothers, a dog, half a dozen cats, a crow my older brother tamed and actually trained to talk, an uncle, one pygmy goat, and a loose cousin who was deaf. My mom was Italian, a little woman full of love and hot tempers. Dad came out of the mountains of Appalachia when he was sixteen, came to California to get a job and meet my mother and get started on his life. She never learned to speak English that well and my dad rarely spoke, so I don't know how they managed to hook up. After a few of us were born, he was gone for some time in the army; other than that, he got through his whole life in the West without hardly speaking.

But all his brothers were talkers, coal miners, too,

and Uncle Charlie was that. He came out to live with my mom and dad before I was born and taught me most all the English I know, though I got some of it from around town too. Words are everywhere like water around a fish, and you just breathe them in like those fish do bits of water, except through your ears instead of gills.

Uncle Charlie lived, quiet, up in his room in the attic and played chess with us kids on the front porch, where he had a big living-room chair pulled out there for himself. Mostly he drank Hamm's beer and smoked Camels and drew a little check he got every month for getting his lungs ruined. He wasn't around much, usually ate his meals at the diner, ghosting around upstairs or down to the saloons to keep tabs on his pool-player friends. "Paolo," he'd say, pronouncing it like "mellow" instead of like "pow-low," the way it should sound. Most outside my family said it "Paul-o." Any way was fine with me. "Paolo," he'd say, shaking his little lightbulb head with those ears that stood up and away from it like a mule, "why you goin' ta give your rook up so easy?"

A rook is a chess piece that looks like the tower of a castle. I wouldn't know I was giving it up. Uncle

Charlie's eyes would glint like sun glancing off shaky water, and he'd take a long slurp from his can of Hamm's to give me a chance to think things over. I would then put my rook or whatever piece I was playing down another way. He'd just move his knight or queen the way he planned all along and pluck up my guy. "I thank you kindly, Paolo," he'd say. "'Cept next time you might wait on my birthday 'fore you go to all the bother givin' me presents." Or something like that. Then he'd chuckle and sink back into his chair. He was only about five foot six and bone-knob skinny. That chair would about swallow him. My dad was bigger.

Actually, he was a giant—over five feet, eight inches. I know what you're thinking, but to my mother's people, that's as big as a giant because that Italian side of my family—my dad called them "the I-talians"—doesn't have one man among them whose head you'd see in a crowd of children. I was walking to the grocery once with my I-talian grandpa and a railroad crossing-guard arm came down, and we just sailed right under and beat that train, and that was the first time I noticed how I ended up short.

We lived one-half block out into the country in a two-story house with electricity and plumbing my dad added himself, it was that old. But it was big and airy with the lights on all the time, as electricity was cheap back then. I suppose as my dad had installed those lights himself, he was proud of them, wanted them burning. We weren't poor since we had plenty to eat, but most looked down on us as if we were. Dad had a job as a fireman for the railroad, which means he sat in the back of a train and read books and was paid enough, so I didn't know I was poor until I was grown and it was explained to me.

Well, of all that tribe, it was me that was the trouble. That's what I'm going to tell you about. I wonder if you've ever been told you were troublesome? "You're a trouble." "You in big trouble." "You want some trouble?" All that. Not a nice thing to hear, but you'll hear lots of it if you're trying to grow up and do it right. Practicing at life is just going to have its troubles. And, no matter what anyone says, it's not good to go against your nature. So, naturally, I stayed out of my way.

It started when I was twelve, back when President Truman fired General Douglas MacArthur, from which I learned anybody can get too big for their britches. Let me tell it to you just the way it was to me then—that is, in 1951.

Rufus—he was the dog—comes around one summer morning after a night out sporting, and he's got a twenty-dollar bill, half-shredded, sticking out of his teeth. My deaf cousin, Billy, is running around making grunts and signs in the air. Nobody pays him any mind except me, as I've seen Rufus's green teeth too. I get a hold of Billy and drag him out back behind the garage and whistle Rufus over to us. He comes, all shaggy and dirty, his white coat gone gray and stringy as the smelliest of mops. Billy pounces on him and wrestles him over onto his back, and I pick the biggest piece of that bill out of his teeth, a little corner with *20* on it. I rub it between my fingers, and it's the real stuff.

"Billy, get off that dog," I say, as Billy is still wrestling him for no reason I know except Billy's small and Rufus is good-natured and lets him. 'Course, Billy's deaf, so saying anything don't do any good. I just grab on to his shirt and tug, most of that shirt washed down past its prime and ripping.

Billy looks at me like he's being waked from a dream and lets go of Rufus and stands up, slapping red dust off himself. Billy's from the Appalachian side of the family, though at nine years old, he's still kind of a runt. Got a face white as a birch and peeling just the same, eyes like old pennies, and a nose that always looks as if it's been running. Has teeth like an undersized rabbit. Those clothes he wore could just as well be buried instead of washed. Nice kid, though. Willing. And quiet, which is an asset in a relative, if you ask me.

"Billy," I say. "Billy, there's more wherever Rufus got this. You understand?"

Billy reads lips. He nods, *Yes,* in a hurry.

"Maybe not enough, though, for just anybody or everybody," I add.

He nods some more, looking at my hand and that torn bit of money. "Why, it might be enough, I can give you some."

He's still looking at my hand, not at my lips, but I know he's in agreement 'cause he looks happy.

"Billy." I grab his head, my hands on both ears, and point him at myself. "This is between you and me for now, okay?"

Sure, he nods, *sure, sure, sure . . . ,* till I stop him with my hands.

"All right, now we have to give Rufus his head and track him back to where he chewed this up."

Now, Rufus is a dog, forever a pup. Was the last of his litter and didn't get all the oxygen a puppy is supposed to get while getting born, so his mind never had the makings it needed to grow. But his body did all the growing he needed. He weighs probably 120 pounds with a head as big as a lion's. I think he's part Saint Bernard and part sheepdog, as those are dogs some of the neighbors have. Half the time he won't sit or stay or really even come on command. He would do it right all the time if he could understand, but as I've said, he can't. Not properly. He is a Mack truck with nobody driving. Usually, he just runs at you full speed, knocks you flat, and then hits the deck and rolls back and forth, tongue lollygagging out. Now, most wouldn't have wanted him, but I know it's things that are different in this world that are fun, and the truth of it is, I loved him from the start and ever after.

Right then, though, was the question of how to get Rufus to go back the way he came.

"Okay, Rufus," I say. I crouch down and hold his head.

He's looking at me, eyes glazed over, sweet and dumb.

"Rufus, you go on now. You go on where you just been." I stand up.

Rufus looks up at me, mouth wide, dog-smiling.

"Go on, boy."

More of that smiling.

"Billy, cut me a switch," I say.

Billy looks at me. Shakes his head. *No.*

I give that a thought, and 'course I know he's right. There's no point putting hurt to a body that don't know why. Fact is, no point in doing such even if it does know. I remember my dad getting mad at a gopher that was eating all my mother's garden squash. He asked around of the neighbors if there was a way to get rid of that pest without trapping it with one of those snap traps that'd break its back.

"Shoot it, you fool," is what I heard one of them say.

"Hmm . . . ," is all my dad said to that, if you count that as talking.

You see, my dad had some New Testament to him too, some of the Quaker. Quakers are quiet folks that take to heart the part of the Bible about turning the other cheek seventy times seven, and I suppose my dad hadn't got up to that count. So he trapped it in this little cage that wouldn't do a varmint any harm. Happened it was a granddaddy gopher, big as a cat, and Dad stared hard at it with that firebrand eye for more than an hour. The gopher stared back for as long as he could, until he couldn't stand it, had to drop his eyes. "That'll do," my dad said. Got up. Let it go.

Next day that gopher and all his kin moved out of the neighborhood. My mother gave up on that garden anyway, as the birds or something else kept after it, and you can't go conversing with all creation.

CHAPTER 2

⟨ornament⟩

"RUFUS," I SAY, GENTLE. "RUFUS, GO ON wherever you please."

He swings his head around to look at Billy.

Billy gives him a sign that I suppose means, *Go on, boy.*

Rufus stands up slowly and trots off. Billy and I trail along, hanging back some so as to give Rufus his own notion of where he wants to go. We go down the block and around the corner, Rufus pointing west as if he's heading somewhere in particular. We're sailing toward town, sure enough, crossing the tracks at Peach Avenue, when we see Mr. Laughlin and his bride rolling toward us. Mr. Laughlin is a junk man of sorts. Wears bib overalls and logging boots. He's skinny with thin arms, hard, though, as those hickory handles on axes. He's bald as a chick with a little bit of dandelion fuzz on the top. Mrs. Laughlin always sits in this wagon fashioned from a shipping pallet with little wheels to it. She's as big as a sea manatee, those slow blubbery creatures, and as plain, but pleasant as anyone's mom. She just sits on that pallet, raggedy clothes they've collected spread all around her like a queen's dress.

"Hey, boys," says Mr. Laughlin, stopping.

"Hello," I say.

Billy nods.

Rufus is reading the news of those rags with his nose. Gives the whole pile a once-over to get the headlines, then burrows in on a part that interests him. He's nosing in hard on some gossip he's found, and it tickles Mrs. Laughlin's bad leg. She has a leg that's withered up. From polio, is what I heard.

"Oh, Rufus, you dear," she says kindly.

Mr. Laughlin says, "Paolo, where you going this morning?"

My name is Paolo 'cause my mother got to name me. My folks took turns: Ernie, Hector, Betsy,

Margarita, Shawna, me—Paolo, Alice-Ann and Aurora, who were twins, George, and Maria-Teresina-the-Little-Rose, as she was the last and my mom wanted to be sure to get all her Italian licks in at the end. Try going around looking like you climbed down from the Appalachians with a name like Paolo. It'll give you an education. My dad said it'd give me patience with folks that are dumb, and being as there are lots of those, I have learned a mighty patience, though I quit all my formal schooling at a young age. You can't do that now, but back then it was nothing. But Mr. Laughlin isn't dumb, and I say, "Well, sir, we're giving Rufus a walk."

"And Billy, too?" he asks, smiling. "He'll enjoy that." I know he's kidding about Billy being like a dog out for a walk 'cause he knows about affliction on account of Mrs. Laughlin's leg and 'cause he's smiling. Mr. Laughlin has teeth that remind me of a picket fence with some of the slats kicked in. Those two are genuine poor, though my dad always says notice how clean they are and Mr. Laughlin shaved up properly, as he always is. Not easy when you live in a shed near the tracks, that cleanliness.

"Yes, sir, we're all going for a walk, I guess."

"Well, I wish you a good day, then, boys," he

says, and leans into this leather harness he's got rigged to himself and the pallet, and the little wheels squeak and they move off very slowly. Mrs. Laughlin turns around and waves with a smile. We watch them till they're almost out of our vision, as they are a thoughtful sight.

We go on our way for another seven blocks or so, until Rufus pulls up just as we're getting downtown. The main part of Orange Grove City starts with Kern and R streets, where the big Cathedral of San Joaquin has stood ever since folks could afford to put up something lasting. A place familiar to us, as my mother drags us there every Sunday and sometimes Wednesday nights, too. It's all brick. Rises up proud, with twin spires that throw shadows for three blocks.

Rufus runs right across its big, wide steps and disappears around the side of it. He runs right down along the row of big, stained-glass windows, us following, and darts into this good-size garden that's all caged, sides and top, too, with Cyclone fencing. It's the Monsignor's garden. He lives a boring life, with no family and all, so the congregation took pity and made it for him, though he is never around there. Half his flock are Irish, like my dad, and after a long day with Mass and tending the sick and such, he has to go see them at Murphey's Place most every evening, which the men don't mind as he is a popular one and would never leave our parish. He likes to help folks rather than boss 'em. Kids like him too, 'cause he wears a cape like Zorro and sometimes will slip you a quarter. He never bothers us about growing up to be priests like Father Tom and Father Dave do. Or, as a matter of fact, like all those others whose names I don't remember did also. Those others moved on after a short stay because the Monsignor's ways troubled them and their modern notions of priesting.

Rufus goes down a short row of snap peas and slips in where we can't see him, excepting his tail, flagging his progress. Down that row we go, and then farther on, where some corn's growing tall, Rufus disappears. I can hear him whining, though, and we can see the stalks shaking, and we follow that shaking, Billy going first, and then out of those stalks of corn an arm shoots, grabs me by the back of my neck!

"Where you going, squirt?" comes the voice of Early Johnson, comes right out of his red, terrible face. I half faint and can't talk, just keep looking at him. Early Johnson is a stout oil drum of a man from

Wyoming. Black hair sprouts from every part of himself. Even the arm with the hand that has me held up like a fish to be measured has a whole nest of spidery hair crawling over it. Hair pokes out the neck of his T-shirt, from his ears and his nostrils. His beard climbs down and curls to a point at his belly. Why, the only bit of his red watermelon skin that shows runs across his forehead and around his eyes. Right now those eyes are hot coals, disturbed and glinting at me.

"Hey, Early," is all I can manage to say. Billy's not showing himself anymore. I don't hear Rufus.

"Don't call me that," Early snaps.

I forgot in my confusion that nobody calls him that to his face. Folks refer to Earl Johnson as "Early" since his job of caretaker for the church has him up every day well before the seven o'clock Mass. They say he is gentle if you leave him alone but never to rile him. In fact, I have it known to me, by way of my older brother Ernie, that his great-great-granddaddy had been a mountain man who got snowed in one winter in the Rockies and got so lonesome he married a bear. All Johnsons have been touchy and hairy ever since, even the women.

I haven't seen any of those. It's my understanding Early came out to California by himself. I have no doubt, though, if the story is true, they wouldn't be at a disadvantage, because circuses are popular and because I suppose there are still places up in the Rockies where women are scarce, and an ugly one will do as well as one that is dainty—one not in need of a regular shave.

"*Mr.* Johnson," I say, correcting myself.

"That's right. You one of the O'Neil clan, ain't ja?" he says.

"Yes, sir."

"Well, now that's straightened out, jez suppose you tell me what you doing in the Monsignor's place?"

And I almost tell him, but I see Billy and Rufus through the cornstalks, stealing out of the gate. Rufus has a face full of mud, and Billy is waving what just looks like might be a five-dollar bill.

CHAPTER 3

"DON-BE WRI-DIK-A-LUZ!" MY GRANDPA Leonardo is saying. He's over to dinner since my grandma is visiting relatives in the old country, and he's sitting at the head of the table. Billy is already there, and I slip in without notice. Early let loose of me without anything more than a "Humph!" Couldn't find Rufus or Billy all day. I looked in every single store, as I figured they'd be out spending my money, but they weren't there or in any of their usual haunts.

My grandpa speaks mostly Italian, but he owns a grocery store where a hundred kinds of people shop, and so you never know what kind of English he'll pick up. Japanese, Mexicans, Irish, Africans, Armenians—just about everybody lives in Orange Grove City. One day he'll call you laddie, and the next, *mijo*.

My dad is sitting at the other end of the table, and the rest of us are spread in between, the women in the middle so as to do the passing of plates. Stony, my brother Hector's crow, is perched in the corner in a big cage fashioned out of chicken wire, eyeballing the eating we're doing and on occasion croaking, "Passa da lasagna."

Margarita has just asked Mom if she can go to the drive-in with Jimmy Assayian.

"Yous all, all yous girls never go with any boys. The boys come talk to your papa, if they wanna talk," Grandpa says, stabbing a fork in the direction of my dad. Grandpa's as dark and round as a chili bean. What's left of his hair is slicked back and shiny.

"She's sixteen, Grandpa," Hector says. At eighteen I guess he feels he's got an opinion, and, truth is, if you're Italian and male and past thirteen, had your confirmation at church, you are a man in my grandpa's sight.

"If-a she's fifty and she has-a no husband, she

don go nowhere without her papa. Or her grandpa. In It-lee a boy talk to a girl by himself, her brothers get-a sticks and they talk-a that boy themselves. That boy, he no bother that sister no more."

"I gotta bat!" says Georgie. He's only six.

"You never mind about that. You still a boy," says Grandpa. But he can't hold his scowling and smiles.

"That's right, you never mind," says my mom, sharply, to Georgie and to Grandpa. She can talk English some, if she really wants to.

I'm still a year from being thirteen, but I say, "This is America, Grandpa."

"Don be wri-dik-a-luz, Paolo. Boy an-a girl is-a boy an-a girl in-a every place." Grandpa says this to everyone and also directly to Margarita.

My mother gives Margarita a little pat on the hand so she won't say anything back.

Maria-Teresina-the-Little-Rose chimes in, "Shawna kisses the mirror. She's prac . . . tiz . . . ing." At four years old it's a big, new word for her.

Always quiet, Shawna turned thirteen in May, sometimes a strange age for a girl, I've been told. She's blond and sweet as a peach, but she goes the colors of a lizard when it's been caught out in the open. She's got one of her cats sitting in her lap, and it's swishing its tail like it's getting ready for trouble. Dad is raising the brow over his strong eye at the information.

Just then Ernie comes into the room, running late. He works full-time for Pacific Gas and Electric because he's grown now, and he comes and goes as he pleases. It pleases him to make every meal, early or late. "So *who* is it gone left those great gooey patches I have to look at every morning I shave?" He's heard everything, you can tell, but he likes to tease anyone he's fond of.

Suddenly, Shawna says, to our astonishment, "I have enjoyed my dinner, Mother, and the pleasure of everyone's company, but I feel a slight headache. I shall retire now." She nods toward Dad and Grandpa in turn. "Father, Grandpapa." Drifts out the room like perfume.

The twins, Aurora and Alice-Ann, whisper busily whatever it is ten-year-old girls whisper to each other.

Betsy laughs. "That girl reads too much. Been at those Brontë sisters' books again." She considers herself grown and shakes her head at Hector, a big reader himself, sitting opposite her.

"Not a bad spell to be under," he says coolly.

"Nun ti preoccupa,' u pat' re' creatur i cuntroll'," Mom says to Grandpa.

I don't speak Italian myself, but know a little by ear. She's saying something like, "Don't worry, their father watches out for the girls." Grandpa shrugs. And dinner goes on in its usual way. Georgie leaves the table to look for his bat. Hector is reaching back to the sideboard to turn the music up on the RCA. We always listen to Tony Bennett or Mario Lanza, or else Hank Williams and Johnny Cash and the like, depending on who is closest to the dial. I catch Dad giving Mom a slow wink with his mule's eye, and she smiles. She's still a pretty one to my dad. They're having their private little moment in spite of the ruckus all around them.

It was a habit they had. I thank God and my dad that there was never a TV in our house. Only the very richest of rich folks had one. We never even got a set when they were cheaper. I would have grown up distracted and missed a lot. We had enough going on without it.

Maria-Teresina-the-Little-Rose claps her hands and climbs up on Grandpa's lap, shouting, "I want a story! I want a story in Italian!"

Everybody groans, "No!" He play-bites her hands with his lips, saying, "I don know mobobby speak Itamam."

"Yes, you do. Yes, you do too!" she cries.

Billy and I see that things are winding down. I give him a nod, and we slip out onto the back porch. We can hear Grandpa starting up with what has to be "Little Red Riding Hood" again: *"C'er na vota, na piccerella ch' se chiamav' Cappuccetto Rosso . . ."*

On the back porch is an old wooden love seat hung from some chains. I sit down, and Billy climbs in too. The light is failing fast, shadows leaking out from the trees and shrubs onto the grass, making a pond of dark. I put out my hand to Billy.

He knows what I mean and hands over the bill. It *is* a five.

In the light of the porch I look it over. It's got dirt on it. I slip it into my pocket for safekeeping.

"Give me the rest," I say.

He shakes his head.

"Billy."

He goes on shaking his head and adds some shoulder shrugging to that.

"You got this in Monsignor's garden, right?"

He nods, *Yes,* and starts making like Rufus digging a hole.

"I see," I say. "Well, we'll have to go back."

CHAPTER 4

B ILLY DOESN'T WANT TO GO. I FORGET HE'S STILL afraid of the dark.

"Billy, ain't nothing different between the day and the night except you can't see as good."

We're out back of our property now, and he's stalling, feeding carrots to Buster, our little goat. Buster has a pen to herself next to a shed off back from the garage. Buster's a girl we get milk from, but we gave her that boy name as she busts out of her pen every chance she gets. Buster gnaws up those carrots, her cheeks bulging like she's chewing tobacco, lids of her eyes half closed with the pleasure. The moon's come up bright as a quarter so that now the grass looks bleached.

"See that moon?" I point him at it, then back at me. "A full moon. We got all the light we need."

Billy looks worried. I can tell that, even in the soft light of that moon.

"Oh, you're thinking about vampires and bats. They love a big moon, but *most* of them are in storybooks, Billy."

He doesn't like my reasoning, I can tell.

"Ain't nobody been murdered in Orange Grove City since Emily Carter went mad and chopped up her sister with her dad's ax. She's living over at the state hospital, Billy. And besides, even if she weren't, she couldn't catch us."

Billy gets eye-wide.

Emily and Frances Carter had been in their eighties at the time. Got to arguing about who would get to open the door if they were to have a gentleman caller, is what Ernie said. Hector tried to tell me both the Carters were alive and well and living in a rest home, but he reads way too much and it sparks his imagination something awful, so, sometimes, I'm doubtful about his thinking.

Billy is starting to tremble.

"Tell you what. Some gypsy tries to jump us and strangle one of us to death, and I'll whack him with Georgie's bat before you're all the way dead."

I'll skip the details, but I will tell you it took me half an hour to get Billy calmed down. I ended up telling him all the money was mine if he didn't come along; and I did have to get that bat, which he insisted on carrying himself.

So we go down to the church without any problem. The lights of those windows are all glowing, mellow as honey. Billy relaxes when he sees San Joaquin Cathedral is still open for business. There aren't but four or five cars—just the Ladies Altar Society dusting up. We go down the side and come up on Monsignor's garden very carefully in the event Early is around. I'm wondering if he has the nose of a bear and might be able to sniff us from a distance. Billy might have been thinking the same because he scoots ahead and goes around the whole cage, peeking in first. He's around where I can't see him on the far side of it when I hear some scuffling behind me, feel my skin go cold. That scuffling is coming loud, then soft, then loud from behind me. I don't want to even look back, but I do. It turns out it's just the dark branch of a eucalyptus the wind's scraping back and forth on one of those galvanized tin rain gutters they got edging the roof.

"Billy," I hiss, "get back over here!" Of course, Billy wouldn't hear me if I hollered through a megaphone. I'm not scared, just a little distracted. And I don't want to disturb those old ladies inside. Billy appears out of the dark in front of me all of a sudden. I jump three feet in the air and come down with a thump.

Billy looks at me.

"Just stretching my legs," I say. Now that he's relaxed, I don't want him getting worried about Early showing up, so I'm setting an example of calm. He knows I'm going out for shortstop next year and got to keep up on my practice.

He's not impressed, jerks his head in a *C'mon* motion, and heads over to the gate. It squeaks something awful when he opens it. I stay put to keep an eye out and protect him if somebody hears. But he's not waiting on anybody and goes in. I'm the one that needs to see what he's along to show me, so I give a last look around and follow. And there in the back of that garden, in the light leaking from those big windows, is a hole somebody's recently filled in. Billy points. I just stare, so he gets down and paddles out the fresh dirt just like Rufus did last night, I suppose. He goes down about a foot, and there's nothing. He keeps pointing at that nothing and shrugging his shoulders, and I finally get his meaning. There was nothing in the hole this morning except that one five-dollar bill.

So I think about that. Rufus chewed up a twenty, and Billy found a five in the same spot this morning. Somebody buried that money and more, I am sure, and then found out that it had been dug at. They must've took it away then in a hurry and missed the one five Billy found. That's my thinking. Probably what Rufus or Billy would tell me if they could.

Then the lights of those windows blink shut. Billy and the world disappear for a minute until the insides of my eyes swell up enough so I can see some. The moon's still out, but the church is as tall as an old three-story mansion, and there's little to see by. Then a black shadow slips past us. Even in that dimness, I can see Billy's eyes bug out like Ping-Pong balls. I grab him by the elbow and start edging toward the gate when we see a little box of light swinging like a brakeman's lantern in some far distance, but it's not, of course, as it's just twenty yards off in that garden and smaller than a raspberry. Billy

sniffs, and I realize it's somebody smoking a cigarette.

"Who's there?" comes a voice I know but can't
place. Don't either of us move, and I stop my breathing. It comes again, and the voice isn't frightened or
angry. "Someone there?" I don't know what Billy
senses, but he starts off in the direction of the light.
He's still got that bat. I decide I might as well get
slaughtered along with him, as I know Grandpa
won't ever let me live it down if Billy gets killed all
by himself.

We go down a row, bordered by the corn there,
and sitting on a little white concrete bench is
Monsignor—well, only his face is hovering there in
the glow of that smoke, as he's got his black cassock
on and blends in with the gloom.

"Monsignor, it's just me, Paolo. Paolo O'Neil. I
got Billy with me too."

Monsignor sees we are taken by the fact that he's
smoking and inhales one more slow drag and drops
that cigarette and stubs it out with his shoe. "Was
your mother inside?"

"No, Monsignor. She's home tonight."

"Well, that's good," he says, and I notice his voice
is hoarse. He seems a little dreamy or confused.

Monsignor has no hair at all and a small round face. Nobody says anything now. Billy starts fingering one of those cornstalks. We've come up near Monsignor, standing almost on top of him.

"You boys want some of that corn?" He pulls back some as we are leaning toward him, examining him.

"No."

"Because you're welcome to it, if you like," he goes on. And I think, *That man's been crying.* I can tell because his voice is like that. Like after you been crying. Monsignor has a complexion so fair, the tip of his nose goes orange at the slightest upset or sniffling. Even in that darkness, we're so close I see it's doing that now.

"Well," he says, standing up, making us step back a little, "you need a ride home? It's time I go to bed. I can take you, though."

Billy is nodding, *Yes,* so I kick him in the back of his calf. If Monsignor shows up with us on the doorstep, my mom will be talking Italian so fast and loud that nobody will sleep for half the night. And she'd start up again in the morning. Dad might forget about the ways of the Quakers.

"No, Monsignor, we're just out looking for

Rufus. Our dog," I add quickly. I'm thinking I'll have to check the weekly schedule for confession to be sure I get Father Dave and not the Monsignor come Wednesday. Catholics have to tell everything bad that they do, have to tell it to a priest, which is the biggest chore of being Catholic, if you ask me. I can see why they sometimes lose out in the church business.

He puts his hand on Billy's shoulder. "Nice bat." Then he says, "Well, c'mon, you boys should be home. Your dog will show up by tomorrow. Might be home right now. In any case, you shouldn't dawdle."

"We're not dawdlers, Monsignor." I'm feeling low about the lying.

He leads us out the gate, and he's looking up at the spires of the cathedral. He goes on looking that way and pats Billy's head and says, "Okay, boys, go on now."

And we do. All the way home I'm thinking so hard, I scarcely notice when we get there. I hardly recognize Jimmy Assayian parked in his dad's Plymouth three doors down from our place. And if Billy didn't point it out, I wouldn't have even seen Margarita there too, cuddled up in his arms, limp as a rainy-day daisy.

CHAPTER 5

THE NEXT DAY MY MOM HAS ME SCHEDULED TO help clean out Mrs. Kanagaki's cellar. She's a Japanese lady from a half block down the road, where the town streets start. There are some around Orange Grove City that still have a grudge about Japanese folks on account of Pearl Harbor, so my mom makes extra sure that we all show the proper respect. I know Mrs. Kanagaki never flew one of those Zeros, those Japanese planes. Hector said she's lived in America her whole life, excepting when she was gone for a spell. That all was before my time, anyway, and I have no feelings about it one way or the other. Actually, I think I would like Mrs. Kanagaki's company more if she had been in the Japanese air force. It is my bad luck that she hadn't, so I know she will be as boring as any old lady. But I don't mind, as my plan is to shuffle things around, get in the way, and be more bother than I'm worth, so as to get sent home and get on with my day.

When I ask how much the job pays, Mom snaps a dish towel across my ear and snatches my plate of pancakes off the table. I give her a look, soulful and sorry as I can drum up, and she puts the plate back. But she says in English, so I know she's not really mad, "You don't fool anybody. Yous jus trouble." Makes me wait till all the others are finished up and out of there before I can eat. My dad has been up and gone three hours, as he has six days of reading to do on his train. He can read through two books just getting to Chicago and the same number coming back. He says it isn't easy with the train bumping along, but he's got used to it. Says that's the way it is with work. You have to take the good with the bad.

Maria-Teresina-the-Little-Rose sticks around to keep me company while I am eating—and to get in some practice sticking her tongue out at grown folks.

Alice-Ann and Aurora take the time to squirrel-peek their heads in on me and snicker. My ear is still burning from that towel, and I'm thinking I'm looking forward to being thirteen and a man and getting some proper respect from women.

I polish off six of those pancakes in a hurry and go on down toward Mrs. Kanagaki's. Billy comes by on his bike. I stop him. "Billy, how would you like to see some Japanese relics?" I say.

He starts backing up that Schwinn bicycle of his and shaking his head.

"I'm going down and see if I can get into Mrs. Kanagaki's basement and see what she's got pack-ratted down there." But I guess Billy knows all about my chore. Isn't any use. He pedals out of there as if I'm covered in measles and catching. I'm thinking it's a shame how young folks are getting so lazy these days. Besides, he and I should be, by all rights, out scouting for my money.

I go up the walk and ring the bell and wait an age for her. Old folks are slow, and their houses reek with a hundred kinds of decay; even the vicious little dogs they keep are all arthritic and smelly. But she opens the door, and she looks bright and healthy. Got a yellow dress on and a little blue apron. Says, "Paolo, it's so very kind of you to come today. Won't you please come in."

I mumble, "Yes, ma'am."

"Paolo, do you like pineapples?" she says. She looks pretty sunny to me, not that old.

"I don't know."

She walks through her living room to the kitchen calling out, "You mean you don't know if you'd like to eat one now or you don't know if you'd like the taste of them?"

"Never ate a pineapple."

"What's that, dear? Come on out here where I can hear you."

I go into the kitchen. It's as clean as new porcelain, the whole place, floors and walls and tile, windows all along one wall looking on to the backyard. She's slicing a pineapple handily as a man and puts mine in a green glass dish and sets it on the table. She sprinkles sugar over it and says, "Sit."

I do and find pineapple with sugar is to my liking. Mrs. Kanagaki talks while I eat. It's pretty clear that she's lonely. You see, Mrs. Kanagaki's husband got pneumonia and passed over when they camped in Arizona for a few years, and her boy, Arthur, was killed in Europe fighting Nazis. She's got a girl in

Tuscaloosa who teaches school. That's why we're doing the cellar today. Got to get some clothes and things out for her girl's new baby.

"What's that baby going to be called?" I ask after she's wound down a little.

"Mary," she says, her eyes sparking for a second. "Pretty name, isn't it?"

So we go down some stairs to that cellar through a door that's outside right near the shrubbery planted close to the house. It's cool down there, though awful with cobwebs and grime.

Mrs. Kanagaki comes right down after me and pulls the chain on a lightbulb and surveys the little cement room there, hands on her hips. "Okay," she says. "I want those boxes pulled off the shelves and stacked neatly. The tools in those cases over there need to be taken out, cleaned, oiled, and put back; oil's in that can. First, though, grab that broom, and let's get this place dusted and swept." She fishes around in a wicker hamper and pulls out some rags. "These will do for dusting." Then she just climbs those steps. "Thank you, Paolo," I hear her voice trailing off.

I'm wondering if Mrs. Kanagaki plays chess, 'cause I know I just got my king checked the way

Uncle Charlie does mine all the time. I go on and dust up and sweep everything into a little pile in the middle of the room. Half those cobwebs get stuck to me, though. Weird that spider spit comes out in all those designs, all silk and glue. I'm trying my own spit, arcing it out toward the walls, when Mrs. Kanagaki comes down those steps with two Cokes.

"Not bad," she says.

I wonder if she means the spit designs or the sweeping, but she doesn't let on. She hands me both bottles of Coke and goes over and hoists one of those boxes down herself. I see she's got a good set of arms. She drags it into the light and opens it. She turns around and says, "Well, why don't we have those drinks now."

I hand her one of the bottles, glad I hadn't started chugging them both.

She takes a dainty little sip and then begins pulling stuff out of the box with her other hand. "Oh my, would you look at these," she says to herself, pulling out one of those baby suits with the moccasins built in and the trapdoor in the butt. She puts her Coke on a shelf and gets busy. Takes out a little dress and some patent-leather shoes, all this Shirley Temple stuff, that little movie-star kid in the old movies. This stuff she drapes over her arm. I down my Coke and am licking my lips when Mrs. Kanagaki stops, drops to her knees, and places those clothes on the floor. She takes out a picture in a wooden frame and holds it with both hands and shakes her head. I come up close behind her and take a look. She's looking at it as if she'd just found the original Declaration of Independence, but it's just a picture of a man standing next to a wooden building somewhere out in the desert. There's a jagged line of mountains in the background.

"That Mr. Kanagaki?" I ask.

She turns around to see me as if she forgot I was there. Got those sparking eyes again, though this time the sparks are sharp. "Yes," she says slowly.

"That him on your camping trip?"

"What?"

"Him camping those years in Arizona."

She looks at me, searching my face for something, then smiles, a smile where the corners of her mouth go down instead of up. "Yes," she says gently. "We weren't camping, Paolo. We were living there. I know I said a camp earlier. The government called it a camp. With the war, people were scared, and they thought we might help the Japanese government in some way.

So they sent us there." She sighs so soft, I almost don't catch it. "Just fear."

I think about that. "Kind of stupid," I say.

"Well, yes. I suppose a lot of fear and what it causes people to do is stupid."

"What was it like there?" I ask, not just making conversation, really wanting to know.

She doesn't say anything, just weighs for a bit whether she wants to talk. Then she says, quietly, "It was hard. But the hardest thing, Paolo, was being mistrusted. Shunned."

"Oh," I whisper, as I don't always know what to say.

She puts the picture back carefully, like it might explode, and stands up, dusting her knees. "Well, these are the clothes I wanted."

"Just that little bit?" I say.

"For today." She lifts a strand of hair back from her face.

"Mrs. Kanagaki?"

"Yes, Paolo?"

"How come if nobody trusted you . . . folks, how come Arthur got to fight in the war?"

"Well . . . later they asked the boys to join. Sent them in their own company, so I guess it was only half trusting."

Then I remember. "Yeah . . . that's right. Hector told me that company got more medals than most."

She looks at me confused.

"Hector, my brother."

She nods her head. "Oh, yes, they fought. Trying to prove themselves. Just boys." Her eyes are a long ways off from that little room in the ground. "Well, Paolo, I think I'm done for today. You can go."

"When you want me to come back?" I say.

"I don't think that will be necessary," she says, already climbing the stairs.

Of course, I know right then, I'm going to stay and clean up proper, oil every one of those tools and get everything stacked. Maybe look at that picture some more.

"Paolo," Mrs. Kanagaki says, turning back at the top of those stairs, "how old are you?"

"I'm twelve, ma'am."

"Yes, I see." And she disappears quickly up into the bright world.

"Hey!" I shout. "You mind if I finish your Coke?"

⟨⟨⟨

CHAPTER 6

Sun comes up like it always does, and I open the front door as usual to see it, and those tools I'd cleaned are all in their wooden case on our porch. It takes me and Billy and Georgie twenty minutes to drag them around the back and into the garage—makes me wonder how Mrs. Kanagaki got them over here in the first place; probably got her gardener or somebody to do it—doesn't help that Maria-Teresina-the-Little-Rose insists on riding on top of that box, crying, "Giddyup, horsies!" First thing I do is take out a wood chisel and a short hammer and chisel PAOLO right across the top, as I have never had something that was all my own. I'm not about to lose it soon as somebody else lays eyes to it.

"You could have done better with a wood-burning kit," Georgie says. Georgie is little but full of opinions. He's Italian-dark, with big doe eyes and long, black lashes.

"We don't have any such kit," I say. I notice persons who don't ever do anything themselves are the first to point out what's wrong with whatever you do. Sometimes I think that should be the dictionary definition of *relative* or *friend*.

"Mr. Chapman at school does," he says, his lips puckered up in disapproval of my handiwork.

"And it's summer and Mr. Chapman's in Arkansas looking after his mother."

"Arkansas?"

"That's right. Mr. Chapman is a person in spite of his being a teacher."

"He has a mother?"

"Yes, it's a fact, Georgie," I say. I'm looking at my name on the toolbox, feeling myself puffing up like a snake on his own territory.

"How come you know everything, Paolo?" Georgie says seriously.

"Can't help it, I guess."

"How long till I know things?"

"Oh, probably when you're twenty-one or twenty-two," I say. "Whenever you get some intelligence."

"How do you know when a person gets intelligence?"

"By talking to them for a bit," I say, smiling at him.

Maria-Teresina-the-Little-Rose is tracing my name with her finger. Billy's just watching.

I go ahead and write out a note that I tack to the box.

These tools are all Paolo's as the box says. If you are Ernie or Hector or Dad, you can use them if you get permission.

I don't want anyone calling me selfish.

"Now, you-all get out of here, please. I'm going to count these tools. I can't count with you talking to me."

They all file out, their faces looking as if Rufus died or something, which he had not.

I open the tool chest and start placing each of those beauties out on the garage floor. Six kinds of hammers, files, drill bits, wrenches, screwdrivers, a couple of coping saws, and too much else to tell. I know a tool is a beautiful thing, fashioned to do just one job, exact. There's a magic in something such as that, as it makes you want to make a thing yourself— just like the man that made each tool especially for its purpose. I'm holding a big Crescent wrench and can almost hear it talking to me, saying, *I haven't tightened a bolt in twenty years; give me a sip of oil and let's go, Paolo,* when I feel somebody looking at me from behind. I'm sure you've noticed that, haven't you? How when somebody puts eyes on your back, you feel it, same as a soft hand. I turn around. It's just Margarita, leaning over carefully, looking close at those tools but not getting too near, as if they will bite her. Typical for a girl.

"Hey, Paolo," she says, real meek. She's especially girly. Always steps clear of us boys, as if we're some brand of animal. Respectful but cautious. A nice trait, I think. Now that she's got it bad for Jimmy Assayian, it's no wonder he likes her back since she has the proper idea of menfolk.

"You have some . . . nice tools there."

She wouldn't know what to say about a tool to save her life. And she ain't out here because she's interested in them.

"You know, last night when . . . ," she starts in.

"Don't worry, I won't say nothing." I'm feeling generous as I am rich at the moment.

"Yes, I know you won't," she stammers.

'Course, if that were true, she wouldn't be talking to me right now. But it makes a little brother uncomfortable having his big sister afraid of him. I've always liked Margarita.

"Jimmy is a nice boy and . . . I'm a nice—," she tries to say before I cut her off.

"Margarita, I don't think nothing about any of that." Margarita is the churchiest one in the family and wouldn't ever do anything she's not supposed to.

"I feel bad that I snuck out like that," she says, "and it would be awful if I've set a poor example for you." She really means it, I can tell. I realize she is more bothered by the idea she might've contributed to the delinquency of a minor than she is I would tell on her.

"You ain't a bad example," I say. And, still in my generosity, I add, "You know, if I have to have a big sister . . . you'll do fine." She crinkles up her forehead at that, so I go on. "Jimmy Assayian is a good guy." That brightens her right up.

"Oh, do you think so, Paolo?"

"Sure," I say. And Jimmy *is* all right. He plays center field for the Orange Grove City High Patriots and has a job working at his dad's bakery. And he's got that Plymouth of his dad's to drive when he pleases.

"He is, Paolo. He is such a nice man," she whispers.

That's a little embarrassing for me to hear, as Jimmy ain't somebody anyone but my grandpa would think of as a man, and I wonder that Margarita is thinking along those lines. In fact, I start remembering about those sister-sticks Grandpa talks about using on boys who talk to your woman-kin. Suddenly, I'm seeing her the way Grandpa must. A somebody that should be looked after. She looks like that girl on the Sun-Maid boxes they pack over in Raisin City.

"Oh, Paolo," she says, and rushes down to kiss me smack on the cheek. That brings me back to my senses, and I push her off me, though it doesn't dampen her opinion of me, as she smacks me another one and stands up beaming.

"Hey!" I yell, as I'm thinking straight again. Then I see, quick as quick, an opportunity. And I take it. "Why don't you make Jimmy teach me to drive?" But she doesn't hear, I guess, as she's gone goofy with her love for mankind and just pirouettes neatly and skips out of the garage. I think I'll have to try her later, when she's more in her senses.

I put each of those tools back, start thinking again, all the while, about my five dollars and the chances of finding the rest. I shove the whole box into a corner and cover it with a tarp, giving it a little pat, as I'm getting closer to being a man—and one with some property at that.

CHAPTER 7

A T THREE O'CLOCK THAT AFTERNOON BILLY
wants the five-dollar bill. He and Georgie are
standing, faces upturned, underneath the oak tree we
have out back, where I'm stretched out on a limb
considering rooftops and clouds and such. I have
determined that most people like gray or brown for
their roof color, but some are of their own mind, and
I can see red, black, and even blue, and it encourages
me that everything and everybody isn't the same.

"Well," I say to Georgie, "Billy wasn't supposed
to say anything about that, so our contract is off, and
it's my five bucks now."

He says something to Billy, and they both look back up.

"Billy doesn't want a contract; he just wants some of that five."

I consider the difficulties of explaining the legal system to a six- and a nine-year-old and also the limits of my knowledge of those matters myself and decide it's a bust. "What's Billy need money for?"

"He crashed his bike and the front wheel is all bent and the tire's flat," Georgie says.

Now, that bike is Billy's true love. His daddy gave it to him before he died almost a year ago, before my aunt went black-sheeping with a plumber from Tarzana. I shinny down from that tree. "I better see it," I say, like a doctor, mindful of my box of tools.

They take me out to the front of our house near the street, where I see that the bike's smashed good. "Bring it around back. I'll see what I can do." They look at me doubtfully. "Just bring it," I say. I head to the garage to get things set out proper. When they wheel in that shiny green Schwinn, I have the tool-box open and the tarp laid down and some of the tools spread neatly upon it.

"You know how to use those tools already?" Georgie asks.

I just look at him like Dr. Scortt always looks at me, looks down over the tips of his glasses and never says anything back. Last time I was there, I asked if the skeleton he has hanging in his room was any kin to him, asked how come he wore a butcher's coat, asked if all doctors used rye whiskey for shaving lotion, and so on. He never said a thing. Doctors keep their business secrets to themselves, I suppose.

So I'm not about to answer any questions. "Billy, hand me the wrench," I command.

Billy looks at me, frowns, picks up a Crescent wrench, and hands it over.

"The smaller one, if you please."

"Why don't you get it yourself?" Georgie asks. I give him Dr. Scortt's look.

Billy sighs but gets the wrench.

"Thank you," I say. I crack the nuts on the front forks and lift the wheel out, setting the bike down carefully. Billy looks nervous, which I let him be, as my powers have been called into question. I lay the wheel on the tarp like a newborn puppy. I examine it and call for more tools. "Georgie, I'll need a pair of pliers, a hammer, some of those clamps, a plumber's wrench, and a glass of iced tea. With lemon."

His mouth is catching flies, and he doesn't move

a muscle. Billy's cradling his bike and not even looking at me.

"Move 'way, Georgie. I'll get them myself." I sort
all that gear out, minus the glass of iced tea no one
has had the kindness to get me, and go back to examining the wheel. I turn it every way I know. It's bent
in half, and the spokes are sprung out like messed
hair. "It's not," I pronounce, finally, with enormous
authority, "fixable."

Billy is reading my lips, and I think he's going to
cry.

"You know what this means, don't you?" I think
to say.

"You got to give us the five," Georgie says.

I give that all the attention it deserves. "It means
we got to go see Early Johnson."

CHAPTER 8

I DON'T LIKE THAT IT'S ALREADY FOUR IN THE
afternoon, but Billy is beside himself and won't
wait on tomorrow, so we head out, Georgie and
Rufus, too. It's a long way to the dump on Orange
Avenue, and it's the hottest part of the day. The good
part, I figure, is that Early might be home by the time
we get there. 'Course, we'll miss dinner. But in summer it doesn't get dark till eight thirty or so. Mom
will quiz us on where we've been when we come
home, but it won't be that unusual that we're late,
except for Georgie. He's never late for meals. But
she'll know he's with us.

The Orange Avenue dump is the only hill any-where around our town. We live in the flattest country you'll ever see. We go out Ash Tree Avenue, past the winery and its sour smells, past L&N Nursery, past Pacific Gas and Electric's maintenance yard, out and out and out farther than out. Georgie gets tired, and I have to give him a piggyback. Rufus's tongue is swinging low. Finally, we see that mountain of trash. It's six city blocks wide and a thousand feet in the air with a little dirt road that winds around it to the top. They take trucks up that road and dump people's junk and come along later with a bulldozer to mash it all down. There's a little pint-size ditch that runs along one side of it, and that has a dirt lane next to it. Down that lane is where Early lives. I've seen it lots of times when I've come with Dad and Hector and Ernie to take big stuff the county garbage truck won't pick up.

We stop there, and I hold on to Georgie's legs to let him dunk his head in that ditch, then Billy. Rufus is thirsty but afraid of the water. I make them stand back and scoot myself off the bank and dip my own head. It's freezing cold.

Feeling a whole lot fresher then, we stalk down the road, kicking up dust. Now, down that road there's clumps of old sycamores, and under one of those is a trailer house with some chicken coops and a woodshed to one side and three or four old cars sunk in the dirt like old rotted molars, and that's Early Johnson's place. Most wouldn't want it, but with those big trees and the little ditch and the quiet in the evenings, I like it. We go up there quiet as thieves 'cause we can tell Early's home—his dented '36 Dodge pickup is parked out front.

I'm glad Early doesn't have a dog and that those chickens are so hot and tired out that they don't hardly flutter when Rufus noses their coop. Anyway, Early has a little cooler hooked to the side of his trailer, and it's going, making just enough racket to cover our noise. We come up close, and I peek into a window that is open but screened. I don't see a thing except a little couch and an old gramophone and a table. Suddenly, we hear singing coming from around the back. It's Early, I can tell, and he's singing "God Bless America."

We all hit the dirt, even Billy, and scoot under the trailer as it is up on cement blocks. Early is still over on the other side, not coming around our way. He's just standing there, singing, and, well, he's making water in little splashes in the dirt. Georgie looks at me astonished, and Billy starts to giggle. I give them a look that says, *Hush up or your life is going to be over,* and they do.

Early finishes up, stops singing at the same time, and clomps up the back steps and into his house. We can hear him moving around above us. Georgie says, "Why does he sing that while he's—"

I put my hand over his mouth and shake my head. All I can think to whisper is, "Early was always a big one for God and country."

Georgie squirms free of my hand, says, "What's that mean?"

"Nothing. Now hush."

We scoot out from under there. I motion Billy to keep hold of Rufus, and I give another peek in the window. Early is starting up that gramophone record player. Starts it, and it plays very soft and scratchy, some sort of piano stuff. Then he moves around in those shadows and ends up sitting on the couch, and he's got a bowl of something. He's spooning it up and off into the shadows. I'm trying to get my mind around that when I see there's an old lady in the corner. My eyes get adjusted so I can just see her in the half dark, and then that spooning makes sense to me. Early is feeding her some mush or something, and she's lapping it up. She's in a wicker wheelchair.

"Gosh almighty!" I say out loud.

"What? What you see?" Georgie whispers.

"I told you to hush," I hiss.

But it doesn't matter, 'cause Early is talking now. Talking to the old lady. I keep on with my peeking.

"Mother," he says, "now how's that, huh?"

She doesn't say anything. She's just working that mush with her mouth. She ain't got any extra hair on her. No beard or nothing. Just frail. I wonder if Early's adopted.

"Mama, I hate that you got to stay out here all day by yourself," Early says. He's being as gentle with her as I ever seen a man be. A whole lot gentler than any bear.

"Someday," he says, "someday, Mama, if my horse ever gets out the gate, you're going to have you some proper nursing and a brand-new, modern record player."

Mama doesn't look like she knows a word he's saying. But she likes the sound of his voice, and she's smiling at that. Early is watching her close as I am. Closer. And they go on like that, her smiling and looking past him and him careful about the spooning and the little rippling sounds of his voice. It's him being sweet to his mom, yet I feel sadder right then than I remember.

I drop down and motion everybody to follow me back along that road. Billy is tugging at me, and Georgie says, "Did you see the money in there?"

"There ain't any money in there," I mutter.

Billy looks like a dark bird took up roost on his head.

Georgie says, "How you know for sure?"

"Just do. Now hush up and let me think." And I try to, but all I can figure is we have some more work to do to puzzle who put that money in the ground and then took it back out. We're tired and hungry and head home directly, and we don't hardly stop all that way at all, excepting once for God and country.

CHAPTER 9

BILLY AND GEORGIE AND I GOT A MEETING planned. We're supposed to have slept on our situation and, come this morning, put our minds together and decide our next move. We all sleep in the same room, and usually I have to stuff a dirty sock or two in their mouths to get any sleep, but not last night, not after all our walking. Those two slept like Rip Van Winkle. They sleep in the same bed, each with their heads in different directions, which usually causes a lot of kicking and horsing around. But last night they looked like they fell out of a tree, both of them, arms and legs every which way, and out cold, so I had to rouse them myself.

I didn't dream a thing except about my dad in the back of his train, reading and saying "Hmm . . ." to himself. He took along *Moby Dick* this time, a big fish story with a man gone crazed hunting that fish all over the ocean. That's what Hector said. It's four days till Dad will be home, and though he always does come home, I miss him all the same. He never says much, but he keeps a steady eye on things. It's like our big house is a ship, plowing through the days, some rough, some calm, and he is the captain that keeps all hands from doing anything foolish or getting themselves drowned. Talking isn't the only way to get something done. He told me that one little bit once, when he heard me giving some kind of instruction to Georgie and Billy.

We meet up at the tree, and this time Billy climbs up with me. Georgie says, "I want up too!"

"George O'Neil," I say, "you have any idea what will happen to me if you fall and end up swallowing your teeth or something?"

"I want up too!"

"Georgie, you're too little."

"I want up too!"

"Go get a rope," I say.

The way I've said it, he's not sure if I'm going to hang him or haul him. Now, my dad would have said nothing no matter how long Georgie kept pestering, but I'm not of that patience.

"Billy," I say.

Georgie has disappeared, gone running for that rope.

"Early don't have that money," I continue. "No way, as he'd already have a decent record player for his mom. I'm thinking it was church money from collections they make on Sundays. I'm even betting Monsignor knows something of it, as he was crying the other night, and he was doing that crying *right in that garden.*"

Billy nods thoughtfully. Being deaf don't make a boy stupid. Billy is a smart one. Fact is, he and my dad always get on.

"Ahhhhh! Ahhhhhh! Ahhhhhh!" It's Georgie screaming.

"What the beeheezus!" I say, startled almost to falling.

Billy sees my excitement and wonders what's up.

"Stop it! Get away! Get awaaaaaay!" Georgie screams.

I slide down that tree like a fireman, my hands scraping, bloody on the bark. Billy drops down behind me and follows me running around in the yard, looking for that screaming.

"Shoo, you devil! Shoo!" I hear from Georgie, around the garage.

We scoot out there quick. Buster is loose, and she—*she,* as you'll remember, Buster is a milk goat—has Maria-Teresina-the-Little-Rose head-butted and pinned to the ground, and that animal's munching her little red pants. Maria-Teresina-the-Little-Rose is giggling, as it tickles, I guess. Georgie is panicked, though, and bouncing around, a little pogo stick of alarm. "Get off her!" he shouts, and gives a run at Buster and tries to kick her. He's dropped the rope he'd gone to get.

Billy gets around the back of Buster to pull on her stubby tail. I go up and grab Maria-Teresina-the-Little-Rose to try and snatch her away. But Buster has a bite of some elastic in Maria-Teresina-the-Little-Rose's pants, and it stretches, so she doesn't come loose from those choppers.

"*Maronn' mia, ch' e' succies', ca!*" It's my grandpa, who's been over for breakfast. Hector, Alice-Ann and Aurora, and my mother and Betsy are all there too, having tumbled out of the house in a rush.

Buster kicks Billy in the stomach, and he goes flying. Hector jumps on Buster's neck, and she swings around with Hector and Maria-Teresina-the-Little-Rose going around too. Alice-Ann and Aurora are screaming in a girly, two-part harmony, and my mom is so scared, she just stands there with her hands on the sides of her face. Betsy's holding her own self with her arms, mouth opened with wonder. Then a lasso slips along and up from the grass like a snake and gets Buster's hind legs, and Grandpa, who's on the other end of that rope, draws up the slack and pulls Buster, who's on her side now, right to himself. Buster lets go of Maria-Teresina-the-Little-Rose. Grandpa whips some more rope around Buster's front legs, and she's laid out there, trussed up and helpless, eyes wild, as if she doesn't know what got into her and how is it that it's still in there, she'd sure like to know. Grandpa's been around animals all his life, and he's used Georgie's rope to good purpose, and quick. He's a marvel to me. But he's not one to suffer fools or goats, either, and I know there's no joke in his heart at the moment.

Mom scoops up Maria-Teresina-the-Little-Rose,

though my littlest sister is still giggling and not hurt, you can tell. Hector's slapping his trousers clean. Billy is sitting up, just winded. Georgie's over by Buster, saying, "Bad girl, Buster. Bad girl."

The twins are still singing till my mom snaps, "That's enough out of you two," and they stop right together on cue, though a little disappointed, as they weren't finished and don't like that that's the end of their noise.

Grandpa says, "This a-leetle goat, she's-a more trouble than-a she's-a worth."

"Oh, she don't know no better, Grandpa!" Georgie cries. That goat is more Georgie's than anybody's. Billy and I do the feeding and the cleaning up, but it's Georgie who thinks Buster's all his, as we got her when he was Maria-Teresina-the-Little-Rose's age, and he took to her right off, like she were a dog.

Mom says angrily to Grandpa, *"Sta capr' adda asci' momo' a ca'! E pe semp'!"* Which means Buster's going to go, I know.

"I'll fix Buster's pen right now," Georgie says. He's already untying her legs.

"I'm-a taking this goat to the grocery right a-now," says my grandpa.

Now, that means he's going to take Buster out to

a place and get her slaughtered and then take the meat to the butcher counter at his store. He put it his way, as the girls are there and he wouldn't spell out the details in front of them. But we all get the idea, especially Georgie.

"Grandpa, you don't need to do that," he says. "I just have to build the pen a little stronger."

But my mother is looking at Grandpa like she isn't going to repeat herself. Maria-Teresina-the-Little-Rose is the most special thing our family owns, and that's in her mind. And in Grandpa's, too. He nods at my mom, some silent radio transmission passing between them. She shoos the twins and Betsy, who is clucking her tongue like a full-grown woman, into the house and goes in with them too, carrying Maria-Teresina-the-Little-Rose, who is clapping her hands and saying, "I wanna nother ride!"

It's me and Billy and Hector and Georgie and Grandpa then. "Get-a yous goat on a leash," he says.

I know he means business.

Georgie starts crying, "Grandpa, you can't do it!"

Grandpa nods at me and Hector. We start getting Buster up and Rufus's leash on her neck. Billy just watches. "George, you's-a boy; you don't cry like a woman 'bout this."

I'm standing there licking my hands that I scraped coming down from that tree and thinking. Even I know a good Italian woman wouldn't cry. I've seen my grandma chop off the head of a chicken without a thought, more than once. In fact, most of the women I know are harder than a man if you push them. But my grandpa is just doing what he thinks is right. Georgie starts wailing awful as any animal. Grandpa can't take that, as it is distressing to him that Georgie isn't aware of his responsibilities as a boy-child.

Hector says, "Grandpa, I've got to go to work." Isn't much that's more important to Grandpa than work, and he dismisses Hector with a satisfied look.

"George, you come a-with me," Grandpa says. "Paolo and Billy will take-a this goat to Mr. Di Cicco's shop."

But Georgie keeps sniffling, and then he just runs out of the yard, which is pretty serious, not obeying my grandpa.

"We'll do it," I say, and that makes Grandpa feel more like the world is still right side up, and he nods to me, slowly.

He looks after Georgie and sighs a big sigh to himself, shakes his head, says to me, "Paolo, you just-a not make for me any more troubles with that-a goat today." And he takes himself into the house. We get ourselves ready to go. Billy and I get Buster and start down the street.

I can hear Grandpa hollering, faint, from out the front window as we are going down the block. "No more troubles, Paolo!"

We take Rufus along so he can practice the herding instincts Hector said he has but has never showed to me. Ain't any different today as he just lollygags around, leaving his usual messages on tree trunks. I suppose that's an easier instinct to practice. Rufus never complicates things. I wouldn't mind being a dog if I had a good family to take me.

Mr. Di Cicco's shop is on the edge of downtown. It won't be much of a walk. We are going along at a good clip, and Buster isn't minding, as she never gets out and it's a treat to her, I suppose. "Paolo, wait up, wait up!" It's Georgie, of course, like I knew it would be.

I act like Billy and stay nosed toward town. Georgie grabs a hold of my arm and says, "Paolo, Buster ain't a mean one. She didn't hurt nobody. Let's take her for a long walk and put her back in her pen. You and Billy can help me fix it up so's she can't ever get out." He's talking fast.

I take my dad's advice this time and stay hushed.

"Billy." Georgie's got himself around in front of Billy and is talking slow now. He doesn't want Billy to miss a word. "Billy, Grandpa will forget all about this in a little while, and you know how to build a pen strong."

I feel a little pang down where my liver should be. I built that pen.

Billy doesn't stop moving, and Georgie starts the crying again.

"Pleeeeeaaaase," he whines.

We keep on.

"Don't anybody love me?" he cries.

Billy and I, being older, know our duty and don't stop.

"Nobody doesn't love me," Georgie cries, and sits down on the sidewalk.

That does it. Billy stops, and, finally, so do I. Then we see Mr. Laughlin and his bride coming down the street. We are glad of the distraction 'cause Georgie is striking our nerves something horrible.

Mr. Laughlin comes up slowly and stops where we've stopped. "Hey, boys!" He smiles. "What are you doing today?"

Mrs. Laughlin's all curiosity from back in her

cart, but she doesn't say anything. She's got her eyes on Georgie. Mr. Laughlin's looking at Buster.

"Gettin' rid of this goat," I say.

"Do tell," he says, giving the studied look country folks always give to an animal. "Don't see a thing wrong with her," he says.

"She eats up people's clothes while they're still wearing them," I say.

"Hah!" Mr. Laughlin laughs. "Why, that's normal for a goat, Paolo."

Mrs. Laughlin says, "Why that boy crying?"

"His goat," I say.

"Oh dear," she says.

Georgie quits his sniffling and comes up to the Laughlins, all red-eyed and sloppy-nosed.

"What you asking for her?" Mr. Laughlin says.

"I don't think we're asking anything. My grandpa is going to sell her at his grocery after Mr. Di Cicco gets her bite-size."

"Ain't many that'll eat goat," says Mr. Laughlin, and though that may or may not be true, it would still mean that some do. "Mr. Di Cicco is bound to charge your grandpappy more to slaughter her than you'll get for her at the grocery," he says, thoughtful.

That word *slaughter* gets Georgie, and he says in

a rush, "Mrs. Laughlin, if I give you Buster, would you promise not to eat her? Ever?" I know he's looking at how big she is and thinking she must have a hunger as huge.

"Now, nobody said anything about givin'," Mr. Laughlin says slowly.

"I wouldn't want to et 'er," says Mrs. Laughlin. "That's a milk goat, son."

I'm doing my own calculations in my head. Measuring out what Grandpa will think if I give Buster away instead of doing exactly what he told me. I know Grandpa doesn't care about anything but getting Buster off the property for good. But he's not one to have his directions defied.

Billy stabs me with one finger in the chest. He's nodding. *Go on and give up Buster to these two.*

Now, I'm in agreement, but that is an easy thing for him to say, as he never gets in trouble for anything 'cause no one ever believes he does anything except what I tell him.

"Mr. Laughlin," I say, "if you keep Buster so as my little brother can come around to visit her when he wants, I'll give her to you. You can get all the milk and cheese out of her you care to."

Now I've said the wrong thing to be sure, as Mr.

Laughlin says back right quick, "I don't want this here goat." Clamps his jaw shut and leans into his harness.

My dad has told me plain enough how the Laughlins never take charity from anybody. They'd haul that shipping pallet and them rags around the world ten times before they'd do that. I don't think there's a thing wrong with taking what's offered if you got trouble. But I know I got no right to trample on Mr. Laughlin's beliefs any more than I'd want him stepping on mine, if I had any. But I say, quick as it comes to mind, "I'll sell her to you for some shirts and pants for Billy."

Mr. Laughlin relaxes into his harness and gives my face a study. He turns around to Mrs. Laughlin, but she's already fishing in those clothes she's got. He looks at Billy, who has brightened up and wandered over to Mrs. Laughlin.

Well, Billy gets more clothes than the three of us can carry. Mr. Laughlin has to tie some to Rufus's back. I think my mom may not like someone wondering why Billy needs clothes from anyone, but she'll take them, I know. Wouldn't insult the Laughlins by giving them back or asking why they gave them. She's got too much keeping her busy to bother about a little thing like this, anyway. Grandpa won't like that Buster doesn't show up at Mr. Di Cicco's unless there is a good reason. So I tell Billy and Georgie that we'll say Buster ran off.

Georgie looks at me, grateful. And a little afraid.

Well, shoot, I decide he's just going to have to learn that it's all right to take on a lie for a good cause. What we're doing is as manly as making steaks out of a goat.

CHAPTER 10

BILLY WILL NOT LET UP ABOUT THAT FIVE AND HIS
bike. We're just rambling along going anywhere
we want. Georgie and Rufus, too. "Billy," I say, "a
person's supposed to save their money in case something bad happens and they need it."

Billy is in front of me walking backward. He
gives me a look. I know he's thinking there is nothing worse than his bike being out of commission and
now is that bad time.

"The idea is that we make our money grow, and
then, well, we could fix your bike or buy a new one
and one for me and, why, Georgie, too."

"How do you make money grow?" Georgie asks.

"Well, I'm not exactly sure, but I hear folks that have it are making it happen all the time."

Georgie thinks on that, but Billy stops so I have to bump into him and stop too. He puts out his hand.

"Billy," I say, "we got to keep hold of the money. It's the most important clue we have. We'll use it to help us find the rest. We got no choice. If we had a clue, I'd fork it right over."

Billy stays put with his hand out.

"All right, Billy, but you are making a terrible mistake. You are only nine years old. You know five dollars is as much as some grown men make in a day?"

He doesn't think nothing about that.

"Okay, I will give it to you soon as we find out what it costs to fix that wheel," I say. "Let's go down to Chester's and see." I step around him quickly, and he runs alongside of me, trying to keep track of my face. Georgie and Rufus tag with us.

We go into town and down M Street, past the courthouse, all done up like a wedding cake of wood, past the county library and Hye Bakery, where Jimmy Assayian works with his dad. Usually, if we stop there, they give us some day-old bread for a dime, but we're not hungry, and I don't want to talk to Jimmy till maybe he's been softened up about giving me a lesson with that Plymouth.

We get to Ventura Street and Chester's Bike Shop and go in. There's bicycles lined up in two rows all down the store. I go directly to a big black Columbia with a spring front fork suspension. Georgie tries to sit on an English Raleigh, a thin, waspy one that reminds me of an old motorcycle, but he's too little to get up. He tries anyway till I tell him to quit before he knocks that whole row over. There are even some genuine Italian racing bikes toward the back that cost almost as much as a car. Rufus is looking in the plate-glass window from out front. He starts scratching at it. "Georgie, go get Chester," I say, and I go over to nose at the window at Rufus and to think.

Chester comes out from the back and says, "What?"

I turn around slowly. "How are you today, Chester?" I say.

Chester frowns. "Well, I'm doing fine. Something in particular you need?"

We have been in Chester's about three thousand times and never bought anything except a tube patch, once. That ain't why he's sore, though. He used to race motorcycles till he took a bad spill and fouled up his knees, and his girlfriend ran off with a Quaker State oilman. He considers bicycles second-rate to motorcycles, and he's just trying to save up enough to go find that girl and sock that oilman. 'Course, Ernie says it's been twenty-two years since she left and she probably ain't worth the looking up at this point. She was a dancer of some sort at the Sequoia Hotel and had a regular list of boyfriends around to see her there on a daily basis and wasn't really Chester's girl in the first place. I do not understand what makes a man go foolish over a woman.

"Well?" Chester says, scratching his green coveralls, then his lean, serious face.

"What if somebody needs a front rim and tire for a Schwinn fixed?"

"This somebody have any money?" Chester has one eye that wanders when he's sore, and that eye is shuttling off to the left.

"Say if that somebody only had . . . two dollars?"

"This somebody any of you know?" Chester's getting suspicious, as he has ended up fixing bikes for kids for nothing, and there's no way he's going to still be young enough to sock anybody for taking his girl if he keeps it up.

"It's just a rumor around our block," I say off-handedly.

"Tell that rumor that if the wheel is bent, he'll need a brand-new one, and that, with a tire, costs eight dollars, thirty-five cents, counting labor."

"We don't need a brand-new one," says Georgie.

Chester is already going to the back room of his shop. "Ain't got any used ones, guys," he says. "And that's not a rumor," he adds.

"How much without the labor?" I call to him.

"Seven fifty," he says, disappearing. "And stay off those bikes!"

Billy looks crushed.

Georgie says nothing.

"Well, it just means we got to do what I've been saying all along."

That doesn't do anything for them.

"Ah, c'mon," I say, and start out the door.

We wander down Ventura looking in at the automotive shops and the paint stores and finally turn back toward home on P Street. We are shuffling along when we see some commotion up by the big playground they have over there. We run on up and see it's a carnival of some kind. Not a big fair like they have in October, just one of those rickety little ones that comes in on a couple of trucks. We set to nosing around right away, though. They got a merry-go-round for small kids and a Ferris wheel not even high as our house and a whole slew of booths and so on.

I stop at one where they got these metal milk bottles stacked up that you are supposed to knock over with a fast-pitch baseball. Costs ten cents for three balls, and if you knock all six bottles off, you get a stuffed panther or monkey or else fifty cents, whichever you please. We watch a high school boy make twelve throws and knock only four of those bottles down. He looks kind of wimpy, though. I know baseball and can do better, but I ain't spending money to prove it.

"Hello, Paolo," I hear in my left ear. I turn and see it's Therese Mueller.

"Oh, hello, Therese," I say.

"Theres*a,*" she corrects me, and looks back over her shoulder at her two ugly friends, who giggle till they're snuffling back snot.

I have no more interest in a girl than I do in working a coal mine like my uncles did their whole lives. But that hasn't stopped Theresa Mueller from following me around this whole past year at John

Muir Junior High. Girls are thinking about boys from the time they get their first doll, I bet. Just part of their strangeness, and they can't help it, but I ain't helping ideas like that myself. Besides, Theresa has more freckles on herself than a person needs, and I have no intention of marrying any girl like that and having babies that look more leopard than not.

"Paolo plays baseball," she says to her friends importantly. They look genuinely impressed, and the back of my neck reddens up. She gives my left bicep a little squeeze, and my whole head blushes up like a geranium. I'll give it to her that she's not as stupid as she looks. But no more.

"Are you going to try to knock those bottles over?" she asks, attempting to bat her invisible redhead eyelashes.

"Nope," I say, my voice catching.

"Oh, why not?" She looks genuinely hurt, and the two ugly stepsisters' heads she's carrying on her shoulders both frown.

"It's not that I couldn't," I say.

The two on her shoulders look at me with their bottom lips sticking out.

Georgie pipes up, "Paolo could knock them down without hardly trying!"

Just then the guy running the booth slides over and puts three balls on the counter in front of me. "Hey, killer, you got a good arm?" He looks to be about sixteen going on thirty-seven, has a tattoo of a frog with a top hat on that's winking from his forearm and skin that's already leathered up. He grins and looks at me, blinking slow like a lizard.

I shake my head.

"Oh, I see how it is. You only *talk* baseball. Don't worry about it, kid. 'Course, if you want to try, it's only a dime."

"Don't you have any money, Paolo?" Theresa whispers to me, closer than I care to have her.

That starts my blushing again, and I feel a little shame on me and just pull that five out from my pocket like I'm not even myself and put it on the counter.

The guy slips it off so neatly, you would think it had never been there and points at the balls. I take them and wind up and let fly. And miss the whole stack of bottles, completely.

The guy says nothing, but the girls are all oohing. I don't look at Billy, but I know what his face must look like. It's on his account, too, that I messed up, thinking about the five that isn't in sight anymore. I take my time with the next and hit the top three squarely, and they topple off like big birds, shot-gunned stone dead. I knock over four of the six the next time and can feel I'm getting my game.

The guy has three more balls already on the counter, and I go through those without a thought and don't get the six this time either. Then he hands me the balls instead of placing them on the counter. Well, I go through that whole five dollars in about eleven minutes. When I'm done, Theresa and her friends drift off, their little voices nothing but wind chimes floating in the air. That Theresa never says anything to me at all. Billy is sitting on the ground with one arm around Rufus. The guy running the booth says, "Move out the way, boys. You come on back tonight. You almost had it."

And I had. All I wanted of women and pride and downgrading myself, of letting down persons like Billy, who looks about to cry. I even start to wondering if when we find all our money, I'll be able to hang on to it long enough to buy one bike, much less a whole store of them. And I sure as heck ain't going to go looking for somebody to sock, unless it's Theresa.

CHAPTER 11

M<small>Y DAD HAS A GUNMETAL GRAY CHEVY STATION</small>
wagon that we pack into like Vienna sausages
in a can. He's back from Chicago, and it's Sunday,
and we're all going to church. All of us scrubbed up
raw, sporting our best clothes. We boys got to take a
bath every Saturday night whether we need it or not.
Not that you could get in the bathroom any other
time even if you were fond of water, as my sisters
consider it their own private office and have business
mysterious to me going in there most of the time. I
got on a red bow tie, white shirt, and salt-and-pepper
corduroy trousers. Georgie and Billy look exactly the

same. Hector and Ernie get to wear long ties like my dad, and the girls are done up in six different flavors of lollipop. My dad's got his good eye in the rearview mirror riding herd on our squirming.

We go in, and the show starts—all the boring stuff first, the part when I read the ceilings and walls. They have the Bible up there in pictures, done a whole lot better than any circus posters, and I never tire of them. Georgie and Billy and I have our heads back on those pews, eyes tracing the heavens, when Monsignor climbs up into his little box to give his talk. We perk up 'cause he makes a new one for every Sunday, and he's better at telling than most movie stars. But today he looks shaky. He starts up and talks about faith and forgiveness, tells how Peter walked on the water out of faith and then how he needed forgiveness by the end of the good book. Says in the end all is made right, made right by the long quiet and peace of eternity.

Then he drops his acting and talks to us direct. "Every Monday," he says, "I make a trip to the bank. I take in all you've been generous with and given of your labor to the church." Then he peters out and just stops. He's staring out over all those heads, and he does that for a bit, people shuffling their feet, the women fanning, a kid crying in the back. Then, like a pinball machine whirring up when it's switched on, he gets his electricity back and goes on in a rush. "Sunday night I believe I had the bag with the money in my car, as I always do. I had had a long day and I was weary, and somehow, I must have dropped it somewhere. Well, I don't really know what I did with it. It's missing. The sad truth of the matter is, I didn't even think to look for it until Monday night." His voice soft, shamed.

The crowd murmurs a low alarm and disappointment. Then, as Monsignor is a real shepherd and doesn't gloss over the facts, he adds, "I had been to see some of my parishioners at Murphey's, and that I regret." He sighs heavily. "That money will have to be made up somehow in order to pay our expenses."

The church is quiet and respectful. They love Monsignor and know him and his ways, and they are all feeling bad for him. I feel bad for him too, but I'm waiting to see if he says anything about any suspicions he might have as to who picked it up. But he doesn't or won't, and, though he's a little man, he sure climbs down looking a lot smaller than when he climbed up. He finishes the service, and we all pour out onto the front steps.

The men gather together in clumps and the women in their groups—the women talking fast and the men slow, but the same things going around. I sit down on the steps with the whole world and the church on my back. I know Billy and I are dead set on finding that money, but I just don't know if I can keep it now.

Billy comes over and sits with me. Georgie is off playing with his little kid friends, running in circles in and out through those folks. Margarita comes over. She's got a lavender flower of a dress on and shiny shoes with short heels. She says, "My, don't we look glum." I don't know what glum is, but it sounds about right for what I'm feeling.

"Well, I thought you just might want to know that Jimmy says you're far too young for a driving lesson." She pauses, and then, as she can't ever keep good news, blossoms out in a smile. "Buuuuut, he says he will give you a ride out to the country and that maybe you could steer around a little. On a dirt road or something."

"Really?" I say, standing up.

"Well, I wouldn't announce it to everyone," she says with a wink.

So I don't. I stay hushed up. I go home and never

say anything all day. When it's time, I go right to bed without any complaining, taking with me my puzzles and secrets. I lie down on my back, cross my arms like I'm dead, keep my mouth and my eyes closed, slick shut, like eternity.

CHAPTER 12

‿

JIMMY TELLS ME TO WAIT OUTSIDE TILL HE'S finished up with work. Two hours in that alley feel like the seven long days of creation. Billy and Georgie get so bored, they play marbles, pitch coins against the brick wall of the bakery, have a dozen wrestling matches, and try to teach Rufus to bark on command. Rufus just lays himself down and falls asleep. I spend my time going over in my head what I know about steering and gassing, which turns out is nothing.

Georgie tells us how his first-grade teacher, Miss Rollins, who is a beauty except for her gapped teeth, has 175 boyfriends. Georgie is only six and has some lying left in him.

"How would you know if she has even one?" I say, as I figure I have some hand in bringing him up.

"Everybody knows it."

"Is that right?"

"That's right. She goes out with one a day and then starts over in December. Gets 'em all in that way."

"She teaching you math like that?"

"I don't know."

"Well, you wouldn't. You wouldn't even know I had a math teacher in third grade never taught us nothing," I say. "She was about six foot two and wore a wig that slipped sideways half the time. She was divorced on account she drank like a sailor and never knew where she was. Carried a cane she brought back from the Solomon Islands. She'd as soon whack you with that cane as not. She looked half elephant and had to have her little boy, Bob, squeeze her shoes on with butter every morning. That made her sound squishy when she walked around the classroom. She got fired one day when she fell asleep and they had a fire alarm, and our class didn't go out."

"What's her name?" says Georgie.

"Oh, let's see, that was . . . was Mrs. Stutz."

"She going to be my third-grade teacher when I get there?"

"'Course not," I say. "I told you she got fired. Married a dairy farmer. Moved to Wisconsin, I think."

"Hey, guys," says Jimmy. He's appeared out that back door with an apron and white gloves of flour still on him.

"Hey, Jimmy!" say Georgie and me.

"Brought the whole crew, did ya?"

"Mom makes me keep an eye on 'em," I explain.

"Well, let me wash up. Say, that your dog?"

We all nod.

He frowns and goes back in.

I think about that frown. "Billy, how about you take Rufus home?"

Billy's been waiting half the day too, and he isn't in the mood to go anywhere. He looks off so he can't read the lips of what I'm saying.

Jimmy comes back out, washed up and ready. "Well, it didn't take you long to take me up on my offer."

"'Course not," I say. Less than twenty-four hours

and some of them right there in the alley where that Plymouth is parked. Jimmy is looking it over. Sees all our handprints on every window, gives me a look, shakes his head.

"Pile in, guys," he says.

Billy and Georgie and Rufus get in the back, and I take the front seat next to Jimmy. We drive through downtown, looking at folks getting off work, catching buses, and buying newspapers from Allen Singleton, a genuine dwarf—in a world of pygmies no less, is what Hector always says. It doesn't take but five minutes to be in the country, and we go along Weldon Avenue for about ten minutes of telephone poles tacked off into the distance. We got the windows rolled down, Rufus with his head out. A little hot wind has kicked up, like it does most times in summer before dusk. It's lifting Jimmy's hair. He has a strong, dark head of hair and a nose bold enough to match.

But Jimmy's not much of a talker, which will be nice for Margarita if they get married. I don't say anything as I am thinking about when he lets me drive and also so as not to bother him. I think how delicious it will be to have free bread for the rest of my life, so I don't want to be a big talker and mess things up for Margarita.

We come to a little service road that runs out into a pecan orchard, and Jimmy bumps off the two-lane and down it, going slow, dust spinning up behind us. He stops the car but keeps it idling and looks over at me.

"I'm thirsty," says Georgie from the backseat.

Jimmy turns around to him. "Don't have anything to drink, kid."

"I'm George," Georgie says.

"Nice to meet you, George."

I realize Jimmy's never really been over to our house and doesn't go to our church, either.

"Okay, partner, scoot over here, onto my lap," he says to me.

"What for?" I say.

"So you can steer."

"I'm too big for sitting on laps," I tell him.

Jimmy chews his lip some and looks at the trees. He looks back. "How tall are you?" he asks.

"Three feet, eighteen inches," I say, adding two in there for good measure.

One of his cheeks bubbles up, and he passes that bubble from one cheek to the other.

"Margarita was real happy you wanted to teach me to drive. Boy, you should have seen her," I add to help him with his thinking.

"That so?" he says back, right quick, unimpressed. He blows that air out through his teeth and then opens the door and slides out in a flash and says, "Move over here. And don't touch a thing until I tell you."

While he's coming around, I look back at the boys and raise my eyebrows six or seven times at them. But they're already perked up plenty.

Jimmy gets in and says, "Okay, clutch is on your left, gas on the right. I'll handle the gearshift, and you don't have to steer—we're just going to go straight."

All of a sudden I'm a little fearful. Jimmy is talking soft, as though I'm in danger.

"All right, push your left foot down and hold the clutch in."

I do.

"Keep holding it," he says, and moves the shifter on the steering column very slowly. "Now keep the clutch in and give the gas a little nudge with your right foot."

I push my right foot down, and that car roars till it's shaking.

"Keep that left foot down and lift up your right foot!" Jimmy hollers.

I do that, and the Plymouth settles right back down.

"Okay, we are going to do that again, and this time just give it a very little gas."

I try that, and the car just purrs some. My clutch foot is getting tired, I can barely see over the dash, and I'm starting to sweat.

"Now let off that clutch very slowly," Jimmy says.

The car jumps forward like a cheetah and then dies. I look at Jimmy. I don't know what he sees in my face, but he's real nice when he says, "Okay, we'll do it again." I see he's patient like Margarita and that they probably get on just fine.

We do it all again and then again and again some more, that car coughing and jumping down that road in little pounces until it evens out and we are sailing along in first gear at about three miles an hour, possibly more. Jimmy says first gear is all I need to know at my age, and I don't argue. We go down about a half mile, where we stop. Jimmy turns the car around, and then I drive it back the way we came. I feel like I'm the captain of the *Titanic* and say so, to which Jimmy just says, "Let's hope not."

I'm even doing a little steering, just a little this way and that. I'm doing so good, even Jimmy seems bored. I give it just this little bit more of the gas, just to get it up to the top of first gear as I'm allowed and to keep up Jimmy's interest. The engine is straining, and Jimmy says, "Well, just go on and push the clutch down." I do and he snicks it into second. "Gas," he says, "gas."

I take that to heart and toe the pedal down halfway and let my clutch foot ease off, and we go sprinting along. Billy and Georgie are clapping, and Jimmy laughs. And all is as fine as it can ever be— that is, till a jackrabbit runs across that dirt lane, and I swerve to the left and we go right into a tree. *Whack!* I let go of everything then, and Jimmy reaches over and shuts the key switch off. Nobody is hurt. I know 'cause he makes everyone get out and checks us over like Coach Morton. He doesn't admonish me, but his face is darker than fireplace soot. The car will still go, and we drive back. This time I go ahead and talk, since I'm nervous and I figure Margarita's chances are pretty slim now, anyhow.

But "Jimmy, I'm sorry," is all I think to say.

"Don't be. I'm not mad." But it's obvious he is, and I guess he knows it 'cause he says, "Well, mad at myself."

"I might be able to help pay for the damage." It just comes out.

"Now, how would you do that?" He's not looking at me, concentrating somewhere out where the right headlight used to be—the smashed front end of that car.

I figure I might as well take the opportunity of his wisdom. Anyone coolheaded as he is must have something to them.

"Jimmy, if somebody lost some money—for instance, a lot of money—who do you think would keep that money if they found it?" I can feel Georgie's ears beating wide open in the silence of the backseat.

"Well, you would be talking about three fourths of the county," he says.

"That many folks would keep it?"

"Why, sure. Probably more."

"But what kind of guy would keep that money if he knew it was needed by them that lost it?"

"Well, somebody that thought he needed it more. And if he wanted it, he'd soon enough think he needed it."

"Yeah," I say, understanding.

"You lose some money?"

"Not exactly."

"What's that mean?" he asks.

I don't say anything more as it wasn't an exact kind of conversation, and I'm thinking how my odds are stacking up like the front end of that Plymouth—fast and in the wrong direction.

CHAPTER 13

HECTOR HAS A JOB WASHING DISHES AT THE Downtown Café around the corner a ways from the church. Sammy Hernandez, his dishwashing buddy, is sick today, and so Hector asks me to go with him to work. You ain't supposed to do any work for wages at twelve, but Hector says he'll give me a dollar and a free sandwich if I help out.

The Downtown mostly takes care of folks from the courthouse and the men from the *County Grove* newspaper. Not that you can't eat there if you are just anybody, as you can. But it isn't a lazy, retired farmer's café; it's always a rush in there before those folks go to work and then again at lunch. A newspaperman is the best sort of job in my opinion. They get to go anywhere they want, nosing a story. They're at every fire, up close at all the automobile wrecks, at the horse races in October, at every crime scene you can feature. One always gets to go up north for executions, too. Ernie says they have to do most of their sleeping at Murphey's, but I think that is fine also. I think it's important to be somebody in this life, and a newspaperman is the best sort of somebody, I imagine. So I would go without the free sandwich and the dollar, but I see no reason to hurt Hector's feelings about that offer and accept.

Hector wakes me at 5:00 a.m., makes me wash up and wear a white shirt. Everything has to be ready by six thirty at that place. We walk down there so early that the world is a hush. Sky pink and tin-colored and still cool. We go in the back door, everything lighted and cozy in that kitchen. "That's Mr. Weinchek. He's the boss," Hector says when I see a man pulling a tray of eggs out of the big refrigerator there; he's old, maybe forty-five, with one little curl on top of his forehead for hair. Mr. Weinchek smiles faintly at Hector and goes on with his work. "Don't bother him," Hector adds.

We put on aprons that they have hanging on hooks there, and Hector motions for me to follow him out into the dining room. "Aren't we going to wash up some dishes?" I ask.

"No one has dirtied any dishes yet. We're going to help Grace."

Grace is a young Mexican woman who waits on the tables. She's small and slim and pretty, with dark flashing eyes. She makes a nice package out of her uniform, is what Hector has said. She sees me right away and laughs, saying to him, "So this is Little Hector? Veeeery handsome."

That isn't especially to my liking, but Hector lights up like the coils on an electric stove and burns bright. We do look kinda the same, though. Appalachian, blond, and short. We put out paper place mats all around and lay silverware down in all the right spots, Hector showing me just how.

Cars begin to pass by out front in the street, and at six thirty sharp Mr. Weinchek unlocks the door. Hardly three minutes pass before people begin coming in. And that place starts spinning fast as a clock in a movie-house dream. Grace takes the orders and the flirting from the men. Mr. Lee, the cook, who wears a white mushroom cap, fries things up lickety-split. Mr. Weinchek mans the cash register and pours coffee, and Hector collects dirty dishes into a gray rubber tub he has on a cart, dumping them for me to put in a big sink of hot suds.

I can see through the swinging door all the commotion and want to be out there talking to the reporters and the lawyers and the clerks or whoever they are, but that isn't my lot.

Washing dishes is more work than I knew, and after an hour I am glad I'm going to see a dollar and a lunch. After a while things slow down out front, and Hector comes back to help with the washing. Mr. Lee lights a smoke and sucks it down with special appreciation. Grace comes by and snaps a towel on Hector's butt as she passes. He doesn't turn around, but he smiles, not at all the Hector that I know at home. Hector is so bookish, he never even talks to a girl that isn't his own sister.

"Can I have that sandwich now?" I ask, seeing as he is in such a good mood and I'm sort of bored.

"Not till after the lunch rush, Paolo. We have plenty to do." He gives me a smirk, shaking his head.

"Can I go out and pick up some dishes or something?"

"No," he says, plunging his arms up to the elbows in the water.

Grace must have heard that, though, 'cause she says, "Little Hector, you want to come with me?" She is standing right there, about to go through that door with the little window set in it so they can see through and not crash into each other going in and out quick like they do.

Hector gives me a cross look and says, *No,* silent with his mouth.

"Sure," I say to Grace.

"Okey dokey," she says, and takes my hand. We go sashaying out, and she takes me right over to a booth by the window where two guys that look kind of doggish and sleepy are lounging.

"Hey, fellas," she says, just as pretty as you please, and she does please 'em. "This is Little Hector. He's getting a tour."

"Well, hello, Little Hector," they say singsong together like a sloppy half of a barbershop quartet.

I stand there looking them over. They look a little worn to me for so early in the morning. One of them takes a loud slurp of his coffee.

"You boys newspaper hounds?" I say.

They guffaw at that, though I don't see why it's funny.

They keep chuckling, so I ask, "Don't you have to be on, getting the news?"

That really breaks them up. I wonder if you have to be half nuts to be a reporter.

"These characters are getting off work, Little Hector, not going to it," Grace says, patting my shoulder. "Stay here a minute, hon, will you?" Another set of guys is waving to her from their table.

"What sort of news you get nights?"

"Sit down, kid," says one of them. A shadow of a beard is already coming out on his face. "Scoot over, Marty," he says to the other.

Marty slides over with a little mock groan. The one with the beard shadow motions to Mr. Weinchek at the register, makes a little spout of his thumb, pours an imaginary thimbleful of nothing into it, and winks. Mr. Weinchek frowns but gets two fresh cups and puts some coffee in them.

"Well, there's all kinds of things go on at night, boy," says Marty.

I see Mr. Weinchek pull a bottle of whiskey from under the counter and uncap it and pour some in that coffee.

"What things?" I say.

Mr. Weinchek brings the special coffee over and puts the cups on the table. Those two nod their heads with genuine gratitude. The one who needs a shave makes a pistol of his hand and fires a blank at Mr. Weinchek in approval. Mr. Weinchek doesn't say anything, just leaves.

"Why, all manner of things, son," he says. "Tell him, Marty."

They both go to slurping their coffee with serious thirst.

"Boy, you just wouldn't believe me if I told you," Marty says.

"I'd believe you," I say.

They give each other a look. "Well, for instance, last night a Mr. Jenkins locked himself out of his car over on L Street." That sets the shadow-of-a-beard one sputtering. "And Mrs. Pluffka had another prowler. That same damn cat!"

They go haw-hawing with gusto.

"You are kidding, right? You two are kidding," I say, 'cause they are so strange, I can't tell for sure.

They sputter into their mugs, and Marty waves me off with one hand. He's young and as thin as an antelope, with a big long head, and he wears a hat, tilted back, and a suit that sags from every place of himself.

"You mean that's all there is to reporting?" I say.

I'm thinking maybe I will have to be a fireman or detective.

They sober up quick. "Well . . . it's not always quiet," says the one.

Then Marty, the other, adds, seriously, "There's fires sometimes, maybe a burglary, or somebody gets into a fistfight."

"Any robberies of late?" I ask.

"Robberies? Well, none at night that I know of," Marty says.

"What sort usually does a robbery?" I ask.

"Well, I don't know." He looks at the shadow-of-a-beard one for help.

"You mean an armed robbery? A guy using a gun and everything?"

"Not necessarily. Maybe just the sort of person that would steal all your money if you weren't watching it."

"Oh, that's easy, kid," says Marty.

"Yeah," says the other one. "It'll be someone that the guy getting robbed *knows*."

They shake their heads all wryness and knowing. And slowly I join them, nodding, wise too now, with that bit of knowledge.

CHAPTER 14

"HOW WE DO THAT?" GEORGIE SAYS. "We'll just have to go by San Joaquin's and follow him around everywhere for a bit," I say.

Billy sits down in the dirt lot, the one behind Alfonso's Body & Paint, where we are the day after my news hunting. "Me and Billy are going swimming in the ditch today," Georgie says.

"You ever see a detective go off by himself?" I say to both of them.

"I never seen a detective, Paolo."

"Well, 'course not. And you won't see much of anything if you are always swimming in the ditch.

And you can't swim in the ditch, anyway, as you'll drown or get locked up in your room half the summer if Mom finds out."

"You swim in the ditch all the time," he says.

"Forget about that. I ain't six and haven't been for over half my life. Billy, what about you, you coming?"

Billy looks like he's going swimming. Has his cut-offs on and a rubber tube. He keeps peeking at me and away like a wise, old rabbit, not wanting to know what I'm saying.

"It's only eight o'clock in the morning. It's not even hot enough to swim," I argue.

Billy shrugs his shoulders.

"Oh, all right, I tell you what. You go with me today to follow the Monsignor, and . . . and I'll give you a one-dollar advance on our earnings."

Billy smirks at that, so I pull out that one-dollar bill Hector gave me yesterday. He almost didn't give it as I ate three sandwiches and two Cokes after we finished with the lunch rush. I asked him for it when Grace was there. He gave it right over.

Billy always was a smart one, and he stands and puts out his hand. As much as it hurts, I give him the buck.

"Now, c'mon, we got to get moving if we are ever going to grow up and be somebody."

"Ain't we somebody now?" Georgie asks.

"Not exactly."

We tromp on downtown. On the way Georgie asks me, "Today is Wednesday, right?"

"That's right."

"Shouldn't we be following Monsignor on Monday, when he takes the money to the bank?"

Georgie is still a kid, but I see he's got a point. He's waiting on me, watching me think. It probably would be better to stalk the Monsignor and his ways on a Monday, but that's five days of waiting. In summertime waiting five days is like five years in a prison of your own self. "Hmm . . . nah. He probably does the same thing on a Wednesday as a Monday," I say. "Didn't think of that, did you?"

"Shouldn't we have gotten up earlier? What if he's already gone for the day?" Georgie says. Now, that was a Georgie sort of thing to say as Monsignor is not an early riser. Not after his nighttime shepherding at Murphey's. Everybody knows that.

"It's only eight," I say flatly.

We go on, stopping once to see Mr. Thu Trong, a shriveled old guy, brown and gnarled as the dry roots he sells in his shop. We rummage around touching and sniffing them all. His sister comes over to shoo us away. She's as old as he is, wears glasses so thick, her eyes look like dead pollywogs in little fishbowls. Just looking at them makes me tear up and blink. She's scowling.

Georgie has a clump of root that looks like a bit of rhinoceros's foot gone bad with arthritis and asks, "What's this one do for you?" We know those roots are for boiling and curing yourself of ailments of all kinds. The Trongs know us well.

"That's for vital energy," I say. Mr. Trong has drifted up like smoke from his chair in the shadows. He wears dark Chinese pajamas like his sister's. She leaves us alone with Mr. Trong but not before mumbling something about us that ain't flattery, I know.

"What's vital energy, Mr. Trong?" Georgie asks, always the curious one.

"It's chi," I say.

"Cheeeee?" asks Georgie.

"Yep, everybody has it," I say. I've spent plenty of time talking with Mr. Trong, as he is strange in a way that interests me. "A tea from that root just helps the chi move through your body."

Mr. Trong takes the root Georgie has and quietly places it back in the bin.

"How much of that tea you have to drink to get your blood moving?" Georgie asks.

"It would depend," Mr. Trong says, finally speaking.

"On what?" Georgie asks.

"On a lot of things."

"Mr. Trong," I say, "you have any roots or powders that help your memory?"

"Yes."

"If a guy lost something and can't remember where, could it make him remember?"

"No, I don't think so." He puts a tiny, dark cigar between his lips and lights it with a Zippo lighter that flares up like a miniature pet dragon he can snap shut on command and does. Just then two men, thin as bamboo and shuffling along arm in arm, come in. Mr. Trong takes a drag and walks ever so slow and painful toward them.

We're already bored anyway and go on and bounce out of there. "How come Mr. Trong doesn't have much of that chi vital energy?" Georgie asks.

"He's a hundred and twenty-six, Georgie," I tell him, which is the truth as I've heard it. "Just suppose he wasn't drinking those teas all the time."

"Oh," Georgie says. "You suppose we ought to start drinking that stuff?"

"I will, myself, when I get maybe thirty or so. You can't start too soon or you might never grow up."

Georgie chews on that and then asks, "You think he has some tea that will make you grow faster?"

"Hush up now, Georgie." I say this as we are at the church. The priests live in the rectory next door. A rectory is a home for priests. It is three stories high and built out of brick with statues on the porch. The only women allowed in are old ones with bad tempers and sour faces who do the cooking and cleaning. Mrs. Bidden qualifies on all counts as she is a mean one who would sweep you right off the porch with the business end of her broom if you were to hang around there. I think Mrs. Bidden believes priests are extra special 'cause they are closer to the Lord, and that's probably true, but it is as if she thinks they are putting in good or bad words about her, so she steps ever so lightly around them. With all her faults, it isn't a bad plan. Anyway, she's out front hosing the walkway with her typical fury, so we skirt down the driveway before she can spot us and go around back where they have the cars parked.

We go in back of Monsignor's black Ford and sit

down cowboy style, leaning back on the grape-stake fence they got there. Now, we are probably the best wait-around-ers you could find in Orange Grove City, but after an hour we get squirmy and are about to quit. I think we will, except we get to arguing about how we are going to follow Monsignor if he is driving his car. Georgie thinks we should hide in the trunk. Billy motions he should take Georgie home and let me hide in the backseat. I check out the back-seat to see if there's room enough for all of us to hide there on the floor. I'm trying the door handle when I hear Monsignor say, "Morning, boys."

I freeze.

"I don't see your dog. Still looking for him?" he says, nothing in his face but how-de-do and good morning.

"We had to leave Rufus home today," Georgie says.

"Why's that?" Monsignor says. He unlocks his door.

"Rufus makes too much racket for detecti . . ."

I grab Georgie by the arm, digging my fingernails to the bone. "Rufus gets lost too easily, Monsignor," I answer. "We left him tied up." Georgie's eyes cross, and he looks like he's going to puke. Billy is just standing there fidgeting with the collar of one of his new old shirts.

"Can I give you a lift somewhere?" Monsignor says, about to duck in behind the wheel.

"Yes, sir!" I say, quick as quick.

His head drops down below the roof of the car as he scoots in and sits, swings around, and unlocks the door. We pile in. Billy can't get his inner tube to fit, though.

"Son, you'll have to let me put that in the trunk," says Monsignor.

"Aw, he can leave it here," I say.

Billy shakes his head firmly. *No way.*

"Okay," Monsignor says, and climbs out, quick, and opens the trunk. Monsignor is still pretty spry for his age. Billy gets out and takes him the inner tube. They snug it in there and lock it up and climb back in the car.

"Boys, there are people waiting on me, so you'll have to go with me for a bit, before I take you . . . Say, where is it I am taking you?" Monsignor has his driving spectacles on, and he looks to me right then, with his nose crinkled into a question, like he probably got beat up a lot as a kid. He's so short that just a little bit of his shoulders and his head show over the seat.

"Well . . . we haven't decided yet," I say.

He frowns but shakes his head and drives off. No, we don't have any summer school, No, we never swim in the ditch, Yes, we know that's a dangerous fool of a game, No, we haven't signed up as altar boys yet, Yes, I will speak to my dad about it, and so on until he pulls up in front of a little house that somebody painted yellow a long time ago. Grass is all dead. One black brick missing like a tooth from the mouth of the chimney top. A pale ghost of a face peering out from behind roll-up paper blinds, brown as tobacco with age. Monsignor gone just long enough for us all three to try out the steering wheel.

He pulls an illegal U-turn and zooms out of there, crosses back over the tracks, drives over to Mayfair Grocery, jumps the curb, and brakes hard. Goes in. Comes out with a big bag he puts in the back with us. Has milk and bread and a stick of salami and a pouch of pipe tobacco and some pepper cheese, we see as we do our detecting. Georgie wants the cheese, but I give him my claw again and he hushes. Monsignor turns on Van Ness, a one-way street he goes up when you are supposed to go down, making for himself a shortcut for a half block and then taking a sharp left. Stops at what used to be a motel but is now a set of run-down apartments with little kids, some still in diapers, playing in a sprinkler that's scissoring water across the parking lot. Sets the groceries there on one of the porches. Just rings the bell and comes back to the car.

Pulls out onto the street, almost hitting a big Budweiser truck, and shoots across town to Veterans Hospital. He swerves a hard right into the driveway, and Mike Callahan, on his Orange Grove City Police Harley-Davidson, who's coming out and just barely misses us, shouts through our open windows, "Damn it, Monsignor, slow down!" Monsignor just waves to him and pulls into the parking lot.

"You know, boys," he says, "Michael never could ring the bells during Mass at the right time, and now he's the one directing traffic." Gives us a wink. Like an elf.

This time he takes us in with him. We get to ride the elevator to the fourth floor. He tells Georgie to push the buttons—up, stop, open. We go down a long corridor and hold up at a door with a window like the one at the Downtown Café, except this door is locked. A man nurse puts his bushy orange eyebrows to the window, sees Monsignor, and opens up. When he sees us, he's about to speak, but

Monsignor cuts him off. "We're going in to see Tommy."

The man nurse looks unsure but lifts his shoulders and says, "Okay, but I'll just tag along." He takes us down a little ways and opens a door and stands outside, letting us go in ourselves.

We go into that room, where a guy is sitting looking out the window at some pigeons there on the ledge, strutting back and forth in the shade. The guy's got on a paper nightgown with snaps at the back and foam-rubber slippers.

"Tommy?" Monsignor says. And Tommy Campbell turns his head to look at us directly. His eyes are pasted on like those pigeons, black and red, sharp and still at the same time. He looks at us—Billy and Georgie and me.

"Tommy hasn't seen his boy in some time," Monsignor says to us as if Tommy can't hear.

Monsignor takes a pack of Lucky Strikes from his shirt pocket and puts them on a little table next to Tommy's chair. Tommy looks at them same as he looked at the pigeons and us. All the same. All new. All nothing. Georgie takes my hand. I try to pull my eyes away from the giant trapped bird that Tommy is.

It's Billy that finally goes over to him, goes over and pats Tommy's shoulder. And Monsignor is quiet and I am quiet and Georgie, quiet. Tommy looks at Billy for a bit and then pats Billy on his shoulder. Billy taps back. Then Tommy smiles ever so slightly. Billy, too.

CHAPTER 15

MONSIGNOR SAYS WE EARNED A LUNCH AND takes us to Coney Island Hot Dogs downtown next to JCPenney's department store. You can get four things at Coney Island Hot Dogs: a hot dog, a chili dog, a glass of milk, a cup of coffee. And that's all. But there is never less than a crowd in there. We each have three chili dogs, even Monsignor. I have to eat one of Georgie's, as he starts looking sick after his second one. Monsignor tells us how Tommy Campbell—that's how I know his whole name—was the best altar boy at San Joaquin's ever. How he played right tackle in high school and married Alice

Thornberg before he went to the Philippines with the Marines. Told us that he was a prisoner of war for three years, and that's why he prefers to live in his room by himself nowadays.

"It's been a long time since the war, though, Monsignor," I say, chewing up the last of Georgie's chili dog. "World War II," I add, to explain.

He looks at me, blinks. "Not so long," he says, shifting his attention to the others spread down the lunch counter.

"Longer than Georgie's whole life. Long enough even I don't remember."

"Yes, I suppose it's good that people forget," Monsignor says, still looking at the folks eating there. "It's yesterday to Tommy," he says softly, and then, turning to me, "I suppose your dad never talks about the war."

"My dad doesn't talk much about anything," I say.

"He used to talk more than most, son." And he's smiling at the thought. "There was a time, nights at Murphey's, when he could keep everyone laughing for an hour or more if he cared to."

I'm all ears, as this is new to my knowing. But he doesn't say anything more about that. In fact, seeing my wonder, he looks kind of embarrassed and coughs some. "Well, you all look as if you're done," he says finally. Billy and Georgie have half that chili smeared on their faces and are smiling at each other. I give them a stack of paper napkins to clean up, and then we sit there, looking at Monsignor with only *What's next?* on our faces.

"Boys, I'm heading back for a nap. Where are you heading?"

Billy and Georgie look at me.

"You could drop us back at the church," I say as offhanded as I can.

Monsignor raises his eyebrows at that. Then starts a little smile that turns into a yawn. "OOOO-kay."

We get back to the church in about 197 seconds, as Monsignor takes his own route and his own speed. I'm grateful he's wearing driving glasses and has a St. Christopher's medal hanging from the rearview mirror. When we are getting out of his Ford, I ask, "Monsignor, whatta you suppose you'll do after your nap?"

He frowns, this time for real, and squints at me curiously, taking those spectacles off. Then he twinkles up in his little Irish way and says, "I have altar-boy practice at four o'clock, and if your mother hasn't got any plans for you—and it doesn't appear that she does—then I want you to be there. Give you a chance to see what it's like." He turns around and goes up the back steps to the rectory directly, but he remembers to say over his shoulder, "Four o'clock sharp, boys."

Now, the fact that Monsignor has played right into our hands, we are glad of; that he is actually thinking of getting us signed on as altar boys is not as pleasing. Ernie and Hector have explained all of this to us. Getting up early on Sundays to work three shifts. Being called in on a perfectly good Saturday morning for a baptism or a wedding. On call for funerals any day of the week, as old folks do their dying at all times. And they said there were little chores to be done in back of the altar. The only fun part was supposed to be the shaking of the little bells at the right point during the service and the lighting of candles beforehand and the snuffing them out afterward. The job didn't pay anything unless it was a wedding and a groom slipped you a dollar, which mostly they didn't. I suppose if you were going to grow up and be a priest or an actor, it would give you a taste of that, but other than that, there just was no future in it.

"I wanna go home," Georgie says.

Billy nods in agreement.

I give it a thought. "Okay, Georgie, you go on home." Billy takes Georgie's hand.

"No, Billy, just Georgie. You and I are still on this case."

Billy smirks, like, *What case?*

"Georgie, if we aren't home by twelve midnight, call the police."

"Why would I do that?" he asks.

"You are too young to know. But you just do it, you hear? Twelve midnight."

Billy is taking an interest.

"The police," I say, "*and* the fire department."

That does it. Billy lets loose of Georgie's hand.

Georgie considers making a fuss, as he's interested himself, but his sleepiness wins out, and he makes off for home, though slowly. Turns around and waves to us once.

Billy and I sit down on the back steps of the rectory. It's nice and shady, and we lay ourselves out on that porch and float off on its cool concrete into sleep. With that big lunch, we probably could have slept a week just like jungle snakes do digesting a couple of small deer if Mrs. Bidden didn't have some devil-cat in her. It's she that brushes our hair with that broom of hers. I wake up right off and open one eye and see that she's trying to tickle Billy's ear. He keeps swatting at the broom straw sleepily, like it's a gnat in his dream. His eyes are racing under their lids. I sit up so she'll see I'm awake and leave Billy alone. That gets her. She doesn't like being caught in her game.

"What's your name?" she cries, her voice cracking high like a ball-peen hammer shattering cold glass. Billy's head snaps up.

"Paolo," I say, giving her the firebrand eye, not letting her off the hook.

"And yours, young man?" she says, swinging over to Billy.

Billy blinks at her.

"Now, don't be smart with me, you little street . . . urchin. You answer me when I speak to you."

I decide to wait things out and not explain. It's interesting to me that she's gone and used a cuss word new to me: *urchin*. Awful. Really neat.

Billy shrugs.

"I will smack you with this broom if you don't speak up." She raises the broom, and I start to think she means it. Billy thinks she means it 'cause he looks around for a way off that porch and sees there isn't one, and he's scared.

I'm about to tell her about Billy when I hear him struggling to say his name. "Wa-gg-he," he finally manages to grunt.

"You think you can mock me? I won't have it. I will not!" She raises the broom.

I'm about to raise my hand.

A booming voice calls out, "Mrs. Bidden, get off that porch!" It's Monsignor at the window. Mrs. Bidden jumps like a puppet that's been snatched up by its strings. "The child is deaf, Mrs. Bidden. Deaf. Do *you* hear me?"

Mrs. Bidden looks like her last chance of getting into heaven is gone. Her eyes well up with tears, and she says, "Oh my. Oh, I'm so sorry." She's looking at Monsignor, who has stepped out onto the porch.

"You might say it to the boy." He's got an Irish fury in him, and I understand then why Notre Dame doesn't use any animal for its mascot. A fightin' Irish is more terrible than a beast.

"I apologize, son," she says to Billy. "I–I," she stammers.

Billy steps carefully past her, off of the porch.

Mrs. Bidden backs away and then scoots around the other side of the building.

Billy is gone.

Monsignor sighs and sits down on the porch steps, where I still am. He looks up at the sky. Touches his head with the fingers of one hand. Those fingers trembly. "Now I've got to apologize to Billy and Mrs. Bidden, I suppose," he says to the sky. I look up there and see only a half-moon, day-faint, making a sideways smile to whoever should look.

CHAPTER 16

SO I MEET TERENCE P. GASTON THE THIRD BY myself. Monsignor goes to get Billy's inner tube out of his trunk and tells me not to wait on him but to go on into the church and introduce myself to the altar-boys-in-training there. They are all one year ahead of me in school, three of them and Terence. He is a pudgy kid with pale, rumpled skin who comes up to me in that cool, dark church and says, "Who are you?"

His buddies crowd me into a wooden pew, and Terence jabs me in the chest with a stubby finger.

I don't say a thing.

"You Irish brat," he whispers. Close in my face. The others cinch up around me like a fishing net and me their catch. Terence isn't that much taller than me, but he outweighs me by forty pounds, at least. Still, I sock him in the nose so hard, he falls back and then trips on the padded kneeler of that pew and goes down on his hands and knees, his nose pumping blood in little spurts onto the tile floor like a rusty faucet that hasn't been cracked open in years. The others just back away and start wandering toward the altar. They know Monsignor will be in any second. I kneel down on one knee and give Terence the hankie my mom always makes me carry in my back pocket. He takes it and rolls over on his back, pressing it to his nose, eyes on me, half scared, half curious.

Then we hear Monsignor clapping his hands as he walks in the front doors, which are about a block away, that clapping echoing around. "All right, let's get to work, boys," he hollers, *oys, oys, oys* echoing after. Terence and I stand up, showing ourselves, and he and I go up to the altar, where the others are standing in the shadows. Terence has got his nose plugged. Monsignor walks down the center aisle to us and gets everybody seated and starts talking.

They aren't going to get to do any practicing of their moves today. No walking around or ringing bells or holding the little gold plate the way they will someday under the chins of folks who are getting Communion.

All he does is make them go over the parts they have to say in Latin. They do all the talking in Latin in Catholic churches 'cause it makes for more interest, sounds like magic spells being spoken, I suppose. Mysterious and very impressive, I think. If God is the great mystery, then he ought to have a language hardly anybody understands. But the altar boys have to talk back to the priest in that Latin whether they know what they are saying or not, and though they only have a few parts, they aren't very good at them. Monsignor is irritated. They haven't done their studying.

Anyway, he doesn't let them go for forty-five minutes to an hour, and then only with a hard warning that they should have their parts down right by next Wednesday or else. Outside he gives me Billy's inner tube, and I pretend I'm heading for home. When I'm following a guy, I don't want him on his guard. I suspect he's only going to go to Murphey's, and I think I need Billy with me to keep me awake waiting around outside of that place. Monsignor's gone off to get his car, but he's taking a long time. I'm just about decided I will get Billy to come with me to follow Monsignor another night when I hear footsteps behind me. I drop that tube and roll my fist up so as to be ready when I hear Terence saying, "Hey, kid, you want a ride home?" I turn around.

Terence is by himself and jerking his thumb toward a white Cadillac parked out front of the church, what must be his dad behind the wheel. Anyway, some guy with a giraffe neck and wearing a beret. I give Terence my meanest look. He smiles crookedly and says by way of explanation, "I thought Irish were all talk."

I curl my arms into a boxing stance. He's not gonna fight me, I know, but I figure I've earned the right to make a show of myself, especially if his crew is all gone and his dad is right there to stop us.

"No, no." He shakes his head. "We're friends," he says, smiling a fat car salesman's smile and putting his hand out. "Shake?" I notice that his rumpled skin is on account of acne. Runs all across his face like those maps with all the bumps to show where the hills are. I go on and shake his hand.

His dad has pulled the Cadillac up alongside us

and opened the passenger door. I don't mind having a chauffeur for once in my life, so I get myself and Billy's tube on in. It fits in the backseat of that car, and Terence and I sit up front with his dad. I give Mr. Gaston my address when he asks, and he nods knowingly at it, and we drive off, that Cadillac rumbling with power.

"You didn't tell me your name," Terence says.

"Paolo." I give him a look that says, *And no jokes now unless you'd like that old valve in your nose opened up again.*

"I'm Terence," he says seriously.

"I know. I've seen you. At school."

"Terence P. Gaston *the Third*," his dad corrects him.

I look at his dad to see if he's playing around, but he's not. I see where Terence gets his snobbiness. Mr. Gaston's got the longest fingers I've ever seen on a man, curled over that steering wheel. He's as skinny as those fingers and tall, and I wonder why Terence is stout and chubby. I know about Terence as his house is right across the street from Yosemite Elementary. It's a big two-story place with a wrought-iron fence running all around it and a sign out on the front lawn that says, GASTON SCHOOL OF DANCE. The second floor is like a gymnasium. I was up there in the third grade when we went over for some culture, went to watch these girls in tights and cotton-candy dresses jumping around and standing on their toes in this fake cardboard forest. I had to hand it to them, as I tried that out at home and found there is no way I know of that you can stand on the tips of your toes. I have respected culture ever after.

Terence's dad was known in Orange Grove City and laughed at behind his back by most every man because he was the one who taught those girls culture. He was from Los Angeles, came up to Orange Grove City when a German movie director tried to marry Mrs. Gaston away from him. She was a beauty that almost got to be in *Gone with the Wind,* and he was kind of dainty, so he brought her up here so as to keep her under wraps out in the boonies or else lose her. That's what folks said, at least, since no one ever saw her. Terence himself was a big shot at school, though. He was rich, it was rumored, and had all the latest stuff: footballs, records, model airplanes—you name it. And he let guys play with his gear if they let him boss them around some.

We pull up to my house. It's just getting dark,

and the lights are all on. Ernie and Hector are on the roof of the front porch, patching a spot where it leaked last winter. Rufus is standing beneath their ladder and barking up at them as if he doesn't know who they are. Billy's lying on the grass staring at that moon, a white sliver of a peeled orange's skin. Grandpa is hanging out of one of the upstairs windows with a Coleman lantern, shouting directions to them in Italian. Mr. Gaston says, "This must be it."

"You want to come over to my house? Tomorrow?" Terence says as I'm climbing out of the car. He looks at me hopefully. His dad narrows his eyebrows down at him. But Terence doesn't see that.

"Sure," I say, slamming shut the big door of that Caddy.

CHAPTER 17

"PROBABLY HAS A REAL PONY OR TWO," I TELL Georgie.

"Think he'll let us ride them?" he says.

"Nah, he keeps them at his stable with all the other animals."

"What other animals?"

"Tiger. Bald eagle. Python snake. I think they sold the elephant to the circus last September, though."

Georgie can't even think of another question, his mind is so busy featuring *that*.

Billy just shakes his head at me. Sometimes I

think Billy believes his job is to be my conscience. But I know my compass isn't off. If Terence doesn't have all those animals, he could have them if he wanted them, so what's the difference? Georgie would never get my point, though—which is that there are some who have it all in this world—without me showing it to his mind in pictures he could believe.

Standing outside the iron gates of Terence's house, ten o'clock in the morning, we can hear a piano going upstairs in the gymnasium of culture.

"How come we don't just go on in?" Georgie says.

"They got this gate for a reason, Georgie. They don't want folks just barging in and disturbing them."

"How they going to know we here?"

"I'm going to whistle Terence out." I put two fingers between my front teeth and whistle good and loud. Nothing happens, so I do it again much louder and long as I can. Then I shout, "Hey, Terence!" a bunch of times, and then Georgie joins me. Billy gets a stick and raps it on the bars of that gate as hard as he's able.

A window in the upstairs flies opens, and Mr.

Gaston sticks his giraffe neck out and tells us something more or less like gosh almighty hush up and please come in and ring the bell for Terence. Then he slams the window. We swing the gate open and go up to the door and ring, satisfied with ourselves that we haven't done so without getting permission. We ring a few times, and finally Terence opens the door in his pajamas. Georgie and Billy give me a look. If we were lolling about in our pajamas at ten o'clock in the morning, my mom would've taken a switch to us. Or at least threatened to.

"Come on in," Terence says sleepily, and we follow him in. That place is all statues and vases and even a little palm tree growing in a big pot like they have in the lobby of the Sequoia Hotel.

We go down a hallway and into Terence's bedroom. He flops onto a big four-poster bed and motions with his hand like a king. "Go on, check it out." We are already policing the place, looking all his stuff over. He has more toys and sports equipment around there than a downtown department store.

Georgie sees a miniature red leather saddle in the corner and says, "This for your pony?"

"What?" Terence says.

"Hey!" I say, interrupting. "Does this float, or is it only for show?" I'm pointing at a three-masted ship, all varnished wood and real canvas sails.

"Sure, it floats," Terence says.

"What kind of ponies could wear that little saddle?" Georgie asks, tugging at my shirt.

"Can we take it down to the duck pond at Roeding Park and sail it?" I ask.

"I don't have to do that. I can put it in my swimming pool."

Georgie forgets about that pony when he hears that. "You got a swimming pool?" he says. "All your own?"

"Of course," Terence says.

"You think your mom will let us go in for a swim?" I ask.

Terence says, slick as you please, no sorrow or anything, "She's dead. She died years ago."

The three of us have our mouths hanging open.

"She wasn't my real mom. I'm adopted."

Our mouths are still hanging.

"What's the matter with you guys? You want to go swimming or not?"

Now I see he's just playing it off, as his voice has cracked. Billy can't hear that, but he's taking a keen interest. Terence jumps off the bed and fishes in his closet and comes out with a pair of orange swim trunks.

"We didn't bring our cutoffs," Georgie says to me, his eyes big with concern.

"You can swim in your skin," Terence says. But he goes into the closet and shuts the door to put on his trunks.

"What that mean?" Georgie says.

"Just what it means. You can't swim anyway, not without your tube, so don't worry about it," I tell him.

Terence comes out of the closet in his bathing suit. His belly sags over the belt line down into a little apron of fat. "Let's go," he says, then, looking at me, since I'm holding the ship now, "and bring that." We follow him outside into the backyard, where there is a sparkling blue cement pool and two tables with peppermint-striped umbrellas. Terence goes over to the diving board and bounces a few times and then dives neatly into the water and swims strongly and expertly to the end, climbs out dripping, seal-wet. "I have three swimming medals," he says to us. We're just standing there. "Well, you going in?"

"Maybe we'll just sail this boat a little," I say.

"Actually, it's a schooner, but okay." He takes the schooner, adjusts the sails and the rudder, and gets down on his knees and launches it. It sits there on top of the water, bobbing in what's left of Terence's waves until its sails catch some wind and it rocks slowly across the pool. Billy and I smile. Georgie runs around to the deep end to meet it, slips, and falls in—*plunk*—headfirst, heavy as a rock. We watch him sink straight down, not even moving his arms. Terence runs a few steps and arcs in a sideways dive into the water, goes straight down, grabs Georgie with one arm, and comes up, breaking the surface. Georgie lets out a loud mewling and starts kicking and swinging, but he's locked carefully in one of Terence's arms. Terence swims with his free arm and his legs to the shallow end, where there are these underwater steps. Georgie climbs out bawling. Billy gets a hold of him and sits him down and hugs him till he finally quiets a little.

"Have my lifeguard certification," Terence says. No one is paying him any mind as we're worried about Georgie. He coughs up a little water, and that scares him and he starts crying again. Takes us ten minutes to get him calmed. Terence is lying on a chaise lounge and wearing dark sunglasses. The schooner is bobbing in a corner of the pool.

"So you guys going for a swim or what?" Terence says.

"I don't know," I say.

"I want to ride your ponies," Georgie says, as he's got all the attention now.

"What is he talking about?" Terence says.

"I want to see the tiger too," Georgie continues.

Terence looks at me, eyebrows raised in a question.

"He heard you have some horses and, well . . . other stuff," I say.

"Kid, who told you that?" Terence says to Georgie.

He points at me.

"Ha!" Terence laughs. He gets the whole thing in a flash because he's older and worldly, I guess.

Billy is giving me my dad's mule eye.

"Kid, I don't even have a dog." Terence laughs again, enjoying my discomfort.

I shoot him a look like I'm considering giving him a punch.

He's not really afraid, but he says, "Ah . . . you see . . ." He crouches down to Georgie. "I had to get rid of my animals. Allergies. Doctor's orders," he says to Georgie, gently.

"What was the name of your elephant?" Georgie asks.

Terence can't help himself then, and he starts haw-hawing till he's crying. He stands up and comes over to me and puts his arm around me like we are long-lost pals. "What was the elephant's name, Paolo?"

"Bessie," I say quietly.

More haw-hawing from Terence. "Yes, that was it." Haw-haw and haw-haw till I shake myself loose of him. He's got me all wet.

"We have to go home," I say.

Terence looks hurt for a second, then mad. "No. No, it's too soon for you to go home." He looks at me, eyes narrowed down. "George doesn't want to go home, do you, Georgie?"

"No," Georgie says. "I want ice cream." Georgie thinks he's at the fair or something.

"See there, Georgie wants to stay." Terence takes us in and dishes up dinner plates of vanilla ice cream, which we polish off in no time, Terence having two dishes himself. After, he makes us go swimming in our skins, though he keeps his trunks on.

Georgie sits on the chaise lounge wearing Terence's sunglasses and holding that schooner.

Billy and I want to paddle around and have fun, but Terence makes us race him so he can beat us every time, till we're too tired to swim at all. Then he makes us towel off and dry in the sun and get dressed and takes us back in the house to show us every single one of his toys again. He keeps asking while watching our faces, "Don't you wish it was yours?" He's not happy till we say, "Yeah" and "Sure" and "Yes, Terence." Then we go upstairs and peek in at the girls doing their torture exercises for a while. Mr. Gaston sees us and shoos us off with a lazy backhanded wave. Terence frowns and takes us downstairs so we can sit on all the big cushy furniture in the living room and watch him try to smoke a cigarette, which he does with much coughing and eye-tearing. Then, finally, Terence P. Gaston the Third lets us go home.

CHAPTER 18

"I'M-A JUZ HAPPY SHE BRING-A HERSELF HOME only," Grandpa is saying to Ernie, who's sitting next to him. As Grandma is back from the old country, we are having a little party for her. Grandpa wouldn't take that trip with her because he was afraid all the cousins and sisters and such would ask him for money. They think everybody in America is rich 'cause we drive cars instead of motor scooters and donkeys.

Grandma is sitting at the head of the table and smiling at everyone. Alice-Ann and Aurora have spent the day stringing colored paper around the ceiling, and Mother and Betsy and Margarita have done all manner of cooking. As it's Friday night, even my dad is here. Billy and I were too tired from being Terence's friends all of yesterday to go down to Murphey's afterward to spy on Monsignor, and tonight there's no way we could miss Grandma's party and don't want to, anyway.

Mother brings in a steaming plate of lasagna, followed by Margarita with another and Betsy with more. Everybody sighs out loud as if they haven't eaten in a month. The women go back and forth from the kitchen, hauling in sausage and garlic bread and cheese and salad and iced tea and wine, for the grown-ups, until the table is piled high. Dad says grace softly and with reverence. Ernie says, "Let the games begin," and everybody dives in, passing plates, pouring glasses full, munching, and saying, "Mmm."

Shawna signs to Billy: *You want some cheese?* Billy nods, but Shawna won't give it until Billy signs: *Yes, please.* Shawna and Hector went to the public library this week and got a book on signing for the deaf and are going to make it their project to teach Billy this summer. When those two bookworms put their heads together on some notion, there isn't any stopping them. Billy will learn signing in no time, that's for sure. I'd hung around this afternoon for his first lesson and had learned some too. It's pretty clever how they have pictures for all the letters and drawings for all kinds of sentences. It isn't really strange at all, once you see the idea of it. Billy saw the sense right off and was genuinely pleased; he even got a little teary.

Grandpa says, from his seat next to Grandma—she looks especially happy to be in his usual seat. "So's you see all the peoples you wanna see?"

Grandma nods and keeps smiling.

"So's you still have-a you money?"

Grandma smiles and ignores him. She is half deaf in one ear, and when it suits her, she tries to sit Grandpa to the side of that ear. She is eating her lasagna, giving my mom her approval with a nod. Italian women take their lasagna to heart. They make everything from scratch and fuss on it as if it's a baby they're making that Mary and Joseph would have to approve of themselves. Mother smiles, but she's watching close to check up that Grandma is really enjoying her chewing, not just pretending. Billy and Ernie and Georgie are using their silverware like forklifts, the mouths of themselves getting loaded up like ships about to set sail around the world.

Hector, who eats slowly, says to Aurora and Alice-Ann, "You two are hardly touching your food."

Together they announce, "We're watching our weight," as they hear women do, I imagine. They are still only ten, thin as new colts.

Grandpa says, "In-a It-lee you no-a get you a husband unless you big. No man wanna leetle girl that she can-a have-a no babies."

My grandma and mom, who are genuine Italian ladies, adjust themselves just a bit more daintylike in their chairs.

"Well, nobody goes hungry in America, Grandpa," Hector says.

"Who says-a so?"

"There is more food grown in this valley than anyplace in the world," Hector says. He's probably right, as he reads enough to be blind.

"Hector, you a-never been around here in the nineteen-a hundred and thirties. You look in that library some more an-a you see," Grandpa says.

"Grandpa, no one starved in the valley in the thirties," Hector says.

"Oh, is-a that-a so? You 'scuse-a me I was-a livin' and not-a readin.'"

"Papa, we are enjoying our dinner," says Mom.

"'Scuse-a me," Stony the crow barks from his

perch in the corner. That sets Dad chuckling in his quiet way. He's not a drinker, but he's already had a couple of glasses of red wine, and his cheeks are bright and his eyes twinkly. I think he still finds pleasure in the Italian ways, though they aren't foreign to him anymore. All my mother's noise saves him from his silence, I suppose.

"I say we read up on what oven-baked crow tastes like," Ernie says.

Hector smirks at him. It's his crow, and it took him three years and a couple hundred books to get it to talk.

"Paolo, are you coming to the Queen of the Valley dance with your friends?" Margarita says to me. That's a surprise. Queen of the Valley is the all-girls Catholic high school. All of us go to public school as it doesn't cost and Monsignor ain't prejudiced. You don't have to go to the Catholic school to come to the church or even be an altar boy. But Margarita has friends at that girls' school. I figure I owe her for smashing Jimmy's Plymouth and blowing her chances of having her own family, so I answer polite.

"I'm in seventh grade."

"Yes, but Queen of the Valley High goes from

eighth to twelfth grade. And all altar boys get in free. I don't think they'd mind if you were only one year shy of thirteen. Actually, only half a year shy, Paolo."

"I ain't an altar boy."

"Wait, that's not what the boy who phoned here this morning said," she says, remembering.

"Terence phoned over here?"

"Yes, Terence was his name. He wanted to know if you were busy today. You were having your lesson with Billy, and Grandma was coming tonight. I told him you'd call him later."

"How come you didn't tell me he called?"

"Well, little brother, I was busy cooking, and I am telling you now."

"Don't give your sister trouble," Betsy clucks, shaking a finger.

Ernie says, grinning, "Got roped in by Monsignor, eh?"

"I ain't an altar boy. I just met some of them over at church."

"You should-a be a good boy for Monsignor," Grandpa says.

Dad swivels his bright eye over to me like a lighthouse picking out a lost boat. My dad was a Baptist until he married my mom, and he still held with

Baptist ways, but he'd been true to his word that he'd raise us Italian Catholic, and he wanted me to be an altar boy, there was no doubt.

"Those boys are all in eighth grade," I say. "Mom, this lasagna is *really* good."

"It's excellent, Mother," Hector says.

"Oh, yeah, and the sausage is terrific," Ernie says, understanding the danger now and trying a little to help out.

My mom looks at me slightly confused. "You mean you can't be an altar boy until you are thirteen?" She speaks slowly when she talks English. She looks at Hector and Ernie, then at me. "I've seen some awfully small boys up there."

Now, if I say, *Yes,* I'll be lying direct and in front of everybody. In fact, everybody has stopped what they're doing and is looking at me. Billy especially.

"It might be," I say weakly. I can feel my dad's eye drilling open a hole in my forehead, a whole crew of my miner uncles pouring in to pick around and find out what's there. My brain itches.

"Well, I think I can get you in to the dance since you will be an altar boy next year. Terence said you even attended a class with him the other day," Margarita says.

Alice-Ann and Aurora make faces at the idea of me in a costume walking around the altar, I suppose, and squeal like the monkey children they are. "Gross!" Then, as they've warmed up, "Gaaaa-rooooss!"

"Well, I ain't going to that dance; all those snobs," Betsy snaps. She wasn't invited, I guess.

"He can be my escort," says Shawna. "I will make a perfect gentleman of him by next week."

Hector and Ernie smile at me—big frauds, those grins.

"Yes, that's perfect!" says Margarita. "I can get you in, Shawna. I just know I can."

"Yes, a perfect little gentleman," Shawna continues, her eyes happy about the thought.

"Won't you be busy teaching Billy his signs?" I say to Shawna, weakly again. "I think it will take a lot longer than one week to gentle me."

Billy signs to me on the sly, *Bye-bye*—as if I'm a lost one now.

"Oh, it won't take much time to see you have a good bath and to teach you a few dance steps," she says.

"That's-a nice you sister show you to dance." Grandpa sighs, groggy with pasta, leaning back in his chair, thumbs in his suspenders.

"I wanna dance!" Maria-Teresina-the-Little-Rose cries out, clapping her hands.

Ernie reaches back and flicks the switch of the RCA, and Frank Sinatra is on. Everybody claps at that. I get up and go over to the phone in the entryway and dial up Terence. The twins trail after me, all ears but pretending they're suddenly interested in a rubber plant my mom keeps by the front door.

Terence answers after one ring. "Terence, being your friend is more chore than not," I whisper hotly.

"What are you talking about, buddy?"

"You haven't got any sisters, 'cause if you did, you'd know you don't tell them anything that isn't their direct business—which is everything—is what I'm talking about." Alice-Ann and Aurora have abandoned their keen interest in rubber plants and are looking right at my mouth as if they are dogs and every word I'm saying a treat.

"Sounds to me like you're awfully scared of girls, Paolo," Terence says.

"I am not; these ain't girls, these are sisters."

He doesn't say anything.

"Well, just don't be calling over here and giving out information on me excepting *to me*."

"What?"

"You went and said I was an altar boy."

"So?"

"Well, what makes you think—"

"Paolo, you were at altar-boy practice."

"Oh . . . yeah . . . right."

"You guys want to come over again sometime?" Terence says.

"Yeah, we'll come over sometime," I say.

The twins have drifted over toward the archway of the dining room and are shooting me little dagger looks. Frank Sinatra is still going. But I don't find any solace in that crooning. I hang up on Terence. I'm thinking I'm in more danger than Stony. Cooked, buttered, and served up by women—beautiful enough to be eaten or married in less than a week.

CHAPTER 19

As Terence is going to the dance and I don't want my sister to be the only one I know there, and as he is still calling every day, Billy and I go over to his house a couple of days later. Billy and I have been having our signing lessons with Shawna in the morning and again with Hector in the afternoon after he gets off work from the Downtown Café, if we are around. Even Dad is reading that signing book.

Yesterday Hector was showing us how to string words together. He'd study the book for a bit, then say a little sentence, Billy reading his lips as Hector made the signs over and over. I'll give you an example:

Hector points at me, then puts the three middle fingers of his right hand up and touches the pinkie to the thumb, making a sort of *W* that he bounces right to left in front of his eyes. It means, *You are weird.* So now, all day, Billy is pointing at me and making his *W's* bounce like jackrabbits across his nose. I'd be mad if he didn't seem to be getting such a big kick out of it.

Shawna already has me in gentleman training, which means making a little bow to her satisfaction and saying, "May I have this dance" before trampling around on her feet for twenty minutes after breakfast, learning the fox-trot. So I insist to Billy that we not go in the Gastons' gate, where we are standing, without making our presence known first, same as we'd done last time. But Billy, not having the burden of being a gentleman, just opens the gate, sashays up to the door, and rings the bell. Terence lets us in, happy as a beaver with a whole forest to chew when he sees us. We sit at the kitchen table while he tells us he's going to call up guys from school and the altar boys from church. He has a little leather book with the numbers in it. He picks out the first one, dials, and says, "This is Terence Gaston the—," and they hang up, I guess, 'cause he doesn't get to finish.

He dials the next number and gets Carleton Sheffield on the line. Carl has to help his dad water five hundred acres of vines and isn't available for a month, is what Terence tells us with a frown when he puts the phone down. Arnie Shurson says his aunt came in from Savannah; he has to show her around. Every one of those boys has some chore or another that anyone in their right mind would want to get out of, but it seems they are content. Anyway, none of them are coming over. The wind's out of Terence's sail. But he looks at us, brightens up, and says, "Where's George?"

Now, Georgie doesn't want to visit Terence the Third anymore, but I decide to say that he has a bad cough and that my mom wouldn't let him out. Billy lets that white lie pass without any of his usual looks. In fact, he nods seriously, like, *Yes, that George is a sick one*.

"Well, let's get out of here, then," Terence says, slapping his thigh.

"Where we going?" I ask.

"I don't know. Let's just get our bikes and cruise around."

"We ain't got bikes. I mean, Billy has one, but the front wheel is busted."

"Hmm, well, I have two bikes. We can take Billy's in and get it fixed and then go."

"Costs eight dollars, thirty-five cents to fix that wheel," I tell him.

"Yes, so?"

"We haven't got it. The eight thirty-five."

"We can go to the bank."

"Won't do any good," I say, shaking my head.

Billy is following all this with keenness, head back and forth, not missing a syllable.

"And why is that?" Terence asks.

"No bank account."

Terence starts shaking with silent laughter. The laugh starts in his hips and dances around his waist, jiggles up to his shoulders, climbs up his neck, and ripples quickly over his face. "*My* bank," he manages to say in spite of the jiggling. Then he looks at us, his eyes big with phony suspense, and crooks his finger. "Follow."

We go from the kitchen through the living room to the hallway, past Terence's bedroom to a large door at the hall's end. Terence turns the big brass handle on that door quietly. We go into his dad's bedroom. It's as big as a living room and has double glass doors that open out to a little flagstone garden on the side of the house. Has a little birdbath fountain and trees all around out there. His room is like what I'd imagine a ship captain would have in his house in Hawaii or someplace. Big wooden chests and black wood walls and plants in pots in the corners. A brass clock on the wall the size of a steering wheel. Terence goes directly to the closet doors of slatted wood and folds them open, and it's another room instead of any closet I know of. He switches on the light, and we all glide in.

There's a wall of shoes in little shelves made the size of each pair, and there's jackets and slacks hung neatly, and his ties are rolled in a rack of little boxed shelves. Terence slides open a tiny drawer in a dresser, built, real cunning, into the wall. He takes from it a wallet and, with his sausagey fingers, slips out a ten-dollar bill. Just then we hear a thump from above and freeze. The ceiling seems to be shaking. Terence looks at Billy, who is looking heavenward and half crouching. "Just dancing up there," he says with a smile. But Billy turns, takes off anyway. We follow, me noticing Terence closing the closet doors carefully and giving the room a once-over look before coming.

Back in the kitchen he says, "Okay, let's get my bikes and go to your house for Billy's."

Billy shakes his head.

"Billy," I say, "if somebody wants to give you a gift, it's rude not to accept it."

Billy signs very definitely to me, *No.*

"Hey, consider it a loan," says Terence, a little annoyed.

"Yeah, Billy, we can pay it back when we get our–" And I stop.

"Get what, your allowance?" Terence asks.

"No. Well, sort of."

"I get my allowance on Mondays. Five dollars a week. How much do you get?"

"We don't get . . . that much." We don't get any, and it hasn't ever occurred to us that we should, as we already have free room and board. Sometimes Grandpa or Monsignor slips us a nickel or a quarter, and my dad always says we're free to hire ourselves out to the neighbors without giving him a cut.

Terence puts the ten dollars in the front pocket of Billy's shirt.

Billy takes it out and tosses it on the kitchen table.

"Hey, if you get *that* much for an allowance, can't we just use some of it?" I say.

"Sure. If I hadn't already spent it."

"Billy won't take this 'cause it's your dad's."

"Well, I'm sorry about that. . . . Well, shoot, then it's mine," he says, and picks it up and jams it into the coin pocket of his jeans. He's miffed.

Billy signs that he wants to go home.

"What's all that gibberish?" Terence asks.

"It ain't gibberish, it's talking. With your hands." I'm about to get mad, and Terence can tell.

"Well, let's just go on my bikes. Paolo, you can hike Billy." He looks at him. "Okay, Billy?"

"Yeah, that'll be good. C'mon, Billy, let's see what kind of bikes Terence has got."

Billy lights up some at this.

Out in Mr. Gaston's garage is an older, red Schwinn with fat fenders and a new mercury blue Bianchi ten-speed racer. "Billy can sit on the back fender," Terence says, pointing to the Schwinn. We move the bikes out of the garage and into the alley behind the house. Terence shuts the gate and then inspects his racer. Billy tries the rear fender of the Schwinn. His weight makes it touch the back tire. It takes all my skill and strength to hold that bike while he climbs up on the handlebars and then to launch us into the street. Terence zips up in front of us, drops behind, cuts circles, and then figure-eights around us, showing off. I'm popping sweat with my labor and because it's overcast and muggy today.

There's only two places to go: out into the countryside, which is only eight blocks away, or else downtown, which is about half that. Terence wants to look at some baseball cleats, so we head down to Blosser's Sports. Terence tells us he can't be bothered with locks or chains for his bikes, so we leave them leaning against a streetlight pole out front and go in.

Amos Zuniga, the clerk, sits on his little stool and puts ten different pairs of cleats on Terence's feet. Terence is being a pain, telling Amos to adjust the laces just so and how he doesn't really like them and all. Amos, who is about seventy, with the cauliflower face of an ex-boxer and still in shape like old boxers sometimes are, is dressed like a referee and getting steamed. Terence is twiddling that ten in his fingers like he's a prince.

When Amos goes off to get one more pair of cleats, I ask Terence, "Aren't you afraid your dad will miss that ten?"

"He won't notice."

"He might," I say.

"Maybe it would be nice," Terence says thoughtfully, "to be noticed. What do you think?"

I give it a moment and think maybe that ten dollars isn't real stealing. Maybe it's some kind of backward way of Terence getting his dad's affection or, at the least, his attention. I decide I don't really know Terence P. Gaston the Third, or even the truth of my thoughts regarding him and will have to put a wait on my judgment. My answer is to shrug my shoulders.

Suddenly, Terence jumps out of his chair and reaches over the glass counter they have there and snatches a silver whistle on a chain and flies back to his seat in a perfect rewind of himself. He pockets the whistle just as Amos comes through the little curtains that lead to the back of the store. He's got a shoe box and a frown. He puts the box down in front of Terence and says, "Try these. You can get them on yourself." He keeps the frown and goes over to look after a kid that is fingering a rack of Louisville Sluggers.

Terence looks at the shoe size printed on the box and, without even opening the lid to look at them, goes to the counter, saying loudly, "Can we get some service over here?" Amos ambles back and rings him up and rips off that register receipt, crossing one hand over the other the way a boxing ref does when he's finished a ten count and is signaling a knockout. In other words, he's through with Terence. He stalks off without even giving Terence a bag. I like Amos. He doesn't have much of a job, but he's had his day and knows it and never takes sass off man or boy. Billy is standing there, and to me, he seems for some reason to be looking after Amos like he is his dad that had passed on and just now come back, only to pass on again. I have to shake him loose of that dream, if that's what it is, to get us out of there.

We drop in on the Sprouse-Reitz five-and-dime, where Terence filches a bag of marbles and some colored chalk. The clerk is old and as brittle as a leaf and tries to shuffle over to grab us, as he's seen it all, but we scoot out of there. We bike along past the police station, and Terence wants to go in and see if the cops will let us look around, but now that I know his fingers are as sticky as frogs' tongues snatching moths, I save Billy the trouble and shout, flat out, "No!"

We have to cross over the ditch on Wishon Avenue going back, and Terence stops us and takes that whistle and chalk and those marbles, too, and tosses them overhand—*pa-plink, plink*—into the current. I don't even ask him why, since I know his answer won't make sense. I wouldn't have stolen that whistle, but I'd have taken it if Terence wanted to give it. I wouldn't have been the one that did the stealing, I tell myself; I would only have used that whistle and not ever sold it, so I don't think I could be faulted for anything. I guess I'm practicing the art of taking care of myself. If I'm ever going to be somebody, I'll have to master that, surely.

Billy is looking where that whistle went down, then he looks at me. He takes his index finger and makes like he's screwing it into the side of his nose. At the same time he nods toward Terence, who is watching the traffic with a faraway look in his eyes. It means, *He's a funny one.*

I shrug like, *Tell me something I don't know.* Then Billy points at the water and does the same screwing of his finger into the side of his nose, which means, *Throwing that away is not a laugh, not funny, but strange.* And I get it! Terence is the one most likely to take something that's not his, whether he needs it or not. I don't know which is the best part—what Billy's figured out or how he just said it to me with his hands. I just know Billy is a smart one. He casts his eyes down, and I understand we should play dumb. We move off together, and Terence has a hold of that far-away look and can't let it go, and I see he's sad about something.

We get back to his house and leave the bikes in the garage. It's late in the afternoon, and I suppose no girls get their dancing instructions at this hour, as his dad's Caddy is gone. Terence invites us to dinner. His house is cold, and he seems now of a lonesomeness pure. He's going to eat a refrigerated, store-cooked chicken, and we are tempted because we never had one of those, but we've had enough of Terence for one day and say No.

Walking home, I start feeling downhearted in the worst way. Terence the Third, is why. I'm thinking that when I find my treasure, I can't keep it without having always this feeling I got now. So I'm downhearted especially. Then I look at Billy, and I know we are more brothers than cousins. We're probably even thinking the same thing right this instant: How do we get into that Gaston School of Dance when there's no Terence the Second, or the Third, around? And what good will it do us if he's already scattered all that treasure like bits of trash off that bridge?

⟨ornament⟩

I FIND OUT WHAT BILLY DID WITH THAT DOLLAR I gave him. The one I got from Hector from my dishwashing day. I find out the night of the dance when he comes up to me and Shawna, head down and blushing, holding out a pink carnation for her. That carnation already has a little bit of black edging some of its petals, so I know he must've got it cut-rate. He thinks a lot of Shawna, what with her teaching him signing. He must, to part with that buck.

You'd think he'd given her a diamond wedding ring the way she acts, face glowing like a picture of a saint and stooping down to give him a hug. A tight hug even though she is gussied up and Billy needing his Saturday bath. I have Ernie's old sport coat on and a starched shirt and my Sunday pants Mom pressed up sharp. I'd asked Hector this afternoon if he didn't think the coat was too big. He'd said, "You'll grow into it." Though I'd doubted I could do much growing by eight o'clock. I didn't.

Also that afternoon I got a strange phone call from Theresa Mueller, the girl from my school who watched me lose all my money at the carnival. She called because she wanted to let me know that as of next year she would be in eighth grade and would be attending Queen of the Valley School. "Well, that's swell, Theresa," I said when she told me.

"What that means, Paolo, is that even though I'm only in the seventh grade, the sisters said I can attend functions at the high school now—as a way of getting to know people, you understand."

"Yeah, sure," I said. The truth was, much as I appreciated the fact that Theresa was going to get to go to Queen of the Valley next year, it was, then, only a few hours until the dance, and I wasn't finished getting ready. I still had to shave what was either the beginnings of a mustache or else some especially stubborn dirt over the top of my lip. And

I wanted to experiment with slicking my hair from left to right because Ernie had told me more Chinese than you could count did it that way, but out here, in the West, it would really set me off in a crowd.

I was thinking this when she finally said, "Well, good-bye." Her voice for some reason kind of like smoke from a damp fire.

"Well, good-bye, Theresa," I replied politely, feeling proud of myself, starting to enjoy this gentleman stuff already.

Still, when it is time to go, I'm a little nervous. At least, I remind myself, I can do some fox-trotting and a little jitterbugging. Shawna has told me I'll do fine. I would have preferred to wait a couple of years to loose my gentleman's powers on womankind, but I am painfully aware it is the powers of womankind that have me standing here now, next to her at the bottom of the stairs so as everyone can give us a look. Margarita is already gone to help set up refreshments with her friends. Everybody says we look fine, except Alice-Ann and Aurora, who cross their eyes at me and make like they have to vomit. I am glad Dad is gone to Chicago as I couldn't take his eyeballing me for better or worse. Uncle Charlie drifts by on the landing of the stairs a little tipsy, stops and looks down at us, then goes on back up the stairs quickly, as if he had a vision and is a little disturbed that he's to the point of having one.

Billy and Georgie want to come along too. We explain how it ain't for little kids and all, but they are not buying it. "Can't we just walk with you till you go inside?" Georgie asks.

"We ain't walking. Terence's dad is bringing us in the Cadillac," I tell him.

"It's only two blocks," Georgie says.

"Don't matter. For your information, gentlemen take their ladies' places in cars." And the fact is, I am glad of that Cadillac for the first time since I've known Terence.

Just then we hear its horn honking, one short and one long, and Shawna takes my hand and we scoot out and down the drive. Terence the Third even piles out and opens the back door so Shawna can get herself in and me, too. Shawna's dress has forty-five slips or more, and it stands up so you can't see her face from the front seat, though that doesn't stop Terence from trying. The whole getup is made out of some kind of poofy chiffon stuff and looks more a fire hazard than anything else.

Mr. Gaston zooms us right over, and we get out

and go up the walk to the cafeteria of Queen of the Valley. The sleeves of my jacket go down past my hands, so I shake loose of Shawna's clutch and shove my hands in my trouser pockets. I got a toothpick dangling from my lip like I saw Richard Widmark do in a gangster movie. Terence the Third is taken with Shawna, I can see. I forgot they are the same age. He puts his arm along the back of her waist like she's his date, which is fine with me. I prefer to be a lone wolf anyhow, and maybe now I won't have to do any dancing at all.

We go inside, where the cafeteria is supposed to look like a swanky hotel ballroom but looks like a cafeteria with some crepe paper and balloons hung about. They do have the lights down some and candles in red jars on the tables, so it isn't too bad. They have Tommy Dorsey going on the phonograph, and about one fourth of the kids are already dancing. I hit the punch bowl right off. I have to roll up my sleeves to keep from making a mess. I snarf down one of the eight plates of Ritz crackers and cheese they have there. Then I wander over to a wall where the other lone wolves are lounging close together. Some of those older boys have leather jackets, Levis, and white T-shirts on, which surprises me. Gives me a little feeling of pity they haven't had any gentling.

I'm eyeing the other wall where the girls without dates are standing staring at our wall like they're a firing squad getting a bead on us. Those girls are all at least a head or two taller than me. But that doesn't stop the uglier ones from giving me sweet little nods. I lean back against the wall and cross my legs and work my toothpick back and forth as if I'm used to better offers. Terence and Shawna are dancing a slow one, and I notice Arnie and Carl are there near me, so they must have got those months of chores finished, the ones they told Terence about, or maybe they are just taking a night off.

A nun in her black gear is walking around making sure nobody is getting too friendly, as this is a regulation dance and not to be enjoyed with too much enthusiasm. I suppose as they never had any boyfriends, it rankles them some to see all their girls in danger of getting one. Suddenly, everyone is looking and pointing at me and laughing. I feel like I'm blooming seven shades of red rose, and I give my outfit a once-over to see if I'm still okay, still gentle. And what do I see? Georgie on the floor tugging at my pants! And right behind me at the window, which is open, are Billy and Rufus—Billy waving to me and Rufus barking. I shake Georgie loose and whisper to him out the side of my mouth to get the heck home. I slog toward the punch bowl like I don't know this kid and give folks a nod and a *Ha-ha, it's quite funny to me, too.*

But Georgie's climbed up me, got hold of my jacket lapels, and I have to give him a stack of crackers to get him to go. He climbs out the window, his pants sagging and some of his rear showing. I decide it's past time I hit the bathroom.

In there some of those older guys are nipping at a pint of Jim Beam whiskey. One is barfing in a toilet. It's so smoky, I can't see the mirror. I blink back my tears, a little overcome with the smoke and the glamour of the moment. One of those boys tells me his name is Rodney Paul and gives me that pint, and I take a swig to show I'm not a kid and spew it right back out all over him. Never tasted anything that nasty other than a teaspoon of some thirty-weight motor oil Ernie made me swallow back when I was Georgie's age and Ernie was trying all kinds of chemistry experiments.

When I come out of there, the kids are jitter-bugging, which is about what it sounds like.

Jumping this way and that and swinging up and down and around your partner as if you are handcuffed to a body you want to be rid of and no matter how you try, you just can't. I see Arnie fling a big Swedish girl off his hip, and she snaps right back to him, tries crawling under him but doesn't get away doing that, neither. What they are doing is more complicated than anything I'd practiced, so I make my mind up I definitely am not doing any dancing.

Charlene Papagni has other ideas, though, and she latches on to me before I can make it back to the safety of my pack. I don't have a chance to make the bow I have practiced, as she just takes my hand and leads me out onto the floor. I'm lucky because the song switches to a slow one. Charlene wraps herself around me tight as an octopus to a rock, so tight that I'm having trouble getting air—she's a big girl and has my head pressed smack to her chest. Only my eyes showing. It's soft and pillowy in there, but I can't remember my steps without any oxygen getting up to my brain. Doesn't seem to bother Charlene, as she leads us around with her eyes closed, soulful and happy.

After that my powers are public, and I have to

dance with every one of those firing-squad girls. I even get so I enjoy it, knowing myself is a comfort to so many. The altar boys of San Joaquin slap my back every time I go over to them and tell me stuff like, "Go on back and pick another, quick, before they get chose by someone else." None of them except Arnie is dancing, but I feel I'm doing as well as anyone there, and it's nice to be treated as one of the guys.

In the end, I get so tired, I sit down with a Vickie DeFendis, who is prettier than the rest, and fall asleep in her pillows. Sister Agatha Ann wakes me, tells me I have had enough of dancing and should go home. I think that's a little ungrateful for all I have done for her plainer girls, but I am ready to go anyway. I find Terence and Shawna, and we go out to the curb, where Mr. Gaston is sitting with the dome light on reading the *Wall Street Journal*. Those two are holding hands and being careful for the welfare of each other—Terence acting like it's a dangerous thing to walk to a car and he has to take special care of Shawna to get her there, and Shawna playing along with that game. I figure I will have to tell her that Terence the Third just looks like a gentleman but ain't the genuine thing. And as I am, why not?

CHAPTER 21

TERENCE CALLS THE NEXT DAY ASKING FOR
Shawna. I answer the phone and can tell he's
got it bad for her. Well, actually, Terence is a lonely
one and probably gets it bad for anyone he might
have a chance with. To my disappointment, 'cause I
wasn't given a chance to do my explaining of what I
know of Terence, I already have instructions from
Shawna that she's not home if he calls. But those
girls at the dance have softened my heart. I feel it's
my duty to help romance along if I can. It's not lost
on me that it's Sunday and Mr. Gaston goes out to
play tennis on Sundays.

I can't betray my sister's wishes, but I don't like the idea of outright lying, either. So I come to the only conclusion I can. "Shawna's not home, but a person can't stay gone all day, if you know what I mean."

I tell Terence when he calls a second time, "Girls like it when a fellow drops by to see 'em, I think." Terence hangs up without answering since he's already gone to jump on his racer, I know.

I grab the Brooklyn Dodgers cap Uncle Charlie put on my bed last night for no reason I know except he does stuff like that. Maybe he thinks I should remember I'm still a boy and don't need any of this fiddling with girls. I go find Billy out front, playing chess with him. Uncle Charlie notices the cap and gives me a one-fingered, shaky salute and smiles to himself. Grandpa gave Georgie a corn kernel the other day, so he's out front of the house planting it where he's buried a cat he found car-mashed in the street. Wants to see if it will make that corn grow faster. Shawna is sitting on the front steps braiding the twins' hair in turns, one of our cats in each of their laps. Alice-Ann and Aurora are afraid Georgie might want the cats for fertilizer and aren't letting them out of their sight.

I say hello to Shawna casually and even hello to the twins, who give me their imitation of fishes pulsing their lips. I get Billy to break off his game. Uncle Charlie doesn't mind as he looks ready to sleep anyway. We go around the side of the house. "We got our chance to check out the Gaston School of Dance," I tell Billy, and give him the scoop. Georgie comes over to us and wants to go this time, as he hopes to find some more cats along the way. I think he'll be more bother than not.

But Billy signs to me, *He could be our lookout.*

Okay, I sign back. Billy smiles 'cause he could have read my lips as usual, but he's pleased that I am paying attention to the lessons too.

We head off taking a slightly different route so as not to meet Terence coming our way. We know we got to be quick, as Shawna is more polite than anything else and will give Terence some time, but she's also capable of shaking him loose faster than Rufus does water after a bath. She'll take a little flattery like any girl, but she's either playing hard to get or really doesn't like Terence. I don't know. Women are a mystery and better left to just wonder at than know.

So we trot over there. We nose in the garage to be sure the Cadillac is gone, and it is. We go through the gate and around to the back of Mr. Gaston's house. We are thinking we might squeeze through the bathroom window they have down that hall, the one I've already noticed is usually half open. But somebody is on our side today since we are trying to right a wrong, I suppose. At least that's what I've told Billy, that we would give the money back to the church, though I haven't decided myself exactly what we'll really do if we find it. Anyway, perhaps we are being given a hand, as those double doors to Mr. Gaston's bedroom are wide open. We go in, all of us, Rufus, too, except Georgie, who is our look-out. He's in front of the garage scouting for Mr. Gaston, with directions to give us a loud whistle should he show up. I don't feel too confident about that because when we left him, he was busy scouting the gutter for a dead bird or frog as we'd found no squashed cats suitable to his purposes on our way over.

We go directly down the hall to Terence's bedroom and open his closet and pull all his junk down from the shelves. We go through his clothes and open any boxes we find. We even check the insides of his shoes. Nothing. Billy scoots under the bed and comes out the other side covered with dust. I check his dresser drawers and his shelves. Then Billy points at Rufus. And darn if that dog hasn't tracked mud everywhere on the carpet. We let him come in as he was the one to have nosed that money in the first place and might do it again, but he's just leaving evidence all over the place and not finding a thing.

Just then we hear whistling coming faint. Then Georgie is shouting, "Hey, Paolo! *Hey, Rufuuuus!*" I'm hoping he's found something dead for his corn and not warning us of Mr. Gaston. We tear out of there, down the hall into Mr. Gaston's room and out those double doors, and hop the fence on the far side of the house. We creep along behind the bushes and peer around the corner of the house. Georgie is across the street, sitting on the curb. Terence the Second is walking from the garage to the house and not even paying Georgie any mind. Mr. Gaston has white tennis shorts on his lean muscley legs and a tennis racket he's twirling in one hand like a fast-gun cowboy. Rufus takes off and goes to Georgie, knocking him flat. Starts licking him all over as he smells that buried cat. We go grab Georgie and head out of there pronto. Mr. Gaston's in the house, probably just now following those tracks around.

On the way home Billy signs, *What now?*

Not wanting Georgie to hear, I push back my Dodgers cap like Richard Widmark would push back his fedora and sign, *Got to beat it out of him.*

CHAPTER 22

A S HE'D BEEN IN THE WAR, IT WAS MY IDEA I'D
go up to get Uncle Charlie to give me some
pointers on interrogating—that is, questioning a
fellow who doesn't want to be questioned. Only
thing is, Shawna grabs me by the hair as I'm trying
to slip up the stairs. "Just where do you think
you're going, sir?" Nobody calls a kid sir unless
they're in big trouble. That's a truth. Just try to
think yourself out of it. You won't.

Fond of my hair and feeling I'm losing some of it,
I stop dead and say, "Hi, Shawna." A thousand por-
cupine pains are stabbing my skull. I twist my face

toward her. "You know, it sure was swell of you to take me to the dance."

"You, sir, told that Terence to come over today, didn't you?"

"I told him you were out like you said. We—*ouch*—were on the general topic of you, I think, but as to inviting him, no—*ouch*—I never did that." And I hadn't. I'd just told him that she wasn't home but would likely show up sooner or later. That girls seem to like company. Something of the sort. He'd done his own calculating.

"Paolo, look me in the eye when you're speaking to me." She's shaking one finger, mad as a hornet and circling around to find the tenderest part of me to sting. I look in her eyes. She punches her face close to mine and won't let loose of my eyeballs, trying to read them like those gypsies at the fair. "Now, you tell me, did you or did you not invite Terence Gaston over here today?"

"Oh, did he come by?" I say, my eyes getting runny, my throat catchy. I think Shawna should be the one I ask about torturing the truth out of a body, not Uncle Charlie.

"He certainly did. And he was under the definite impression that you'd asked him over."

"Uh . . . you know, I did say I needed to talk to him, but I thought he understood I was going over to his house to talk."

"Are you saying you were over to his house just now?"

"Oh . . ."

She gives my hair another little yank. "Where exactly have you been?" Then adds, "And, for that matter, what was it that was so important you had to go over to discuss it with Terence at his house and not on the phone?"

"Well . . . you see . . . well, it was my idea the altar boys should wash folks' cars to raise money for Early Johnson's mom." Comes out all of its own. Even sounds to me as if I believe it. Maybe like a dream you have that's a message of truth you don't think directly but comes out of you just the same. Anyway, it stops her. She lets go my hair, and her eyes go quiet and curious, right off.

"What's wrong with Earl Johnson's mother?" she says, voice soft, concerned.

"Just old. And lonely. Early wants her to have a phonograph record player."

"He does? How do you know that?"

"Monsignor told me." I am in deep now and

treading water, afraid I might be heading over a waterfall any second. Hector told me they got a river in hell.

"I see." She sits down on the stairs, puts her chin in her hands.

"Well, I got lots to do," I say, stepping by her.

"Where did you go, then, as Terence was here and not at his home?"

"Oh, looking for some others to talk it up with."

"So are you boys going to do it?"

"Could be," I say.

"Could be," she says, looking up, eyes hot. "You should do it. I could get my friends to help too." Then she stops and says, "Paolo, where'd you get this idea about washing cars for people?"

"I don't know."

"Paolo, people wash their own cars on Saturday or Sunday afternoons. And not everybody has one, you know. I have my doubts about anyone paying someone to do it for them."

I have the same doubts myself now that I think of it, but I say, "Why not?" as I ain't going to do any such thing in any case.

"Well, it's just not done, that's all."

"Okay. You know, Early's mom already has an old gramophone anyway."

"But . . . ," she says, all latched on to the idea as if it were hers and real, "what if we did it at a gas station? People get their windows washed while they're there. They might want their cars washed too."

"I don't know. What would we charge?" I ask.

"Perhaps fifty cents?"

"Shawna, that's more than they'd pay for two gallons of gas."

"Okay, so we ask twenty-five. You know, it definitely is an original idea. Maybe it's so original that no one will buy it, or maybe it's just so original that it will work better than we could ever dream." Shawna is a girl and gets her imagination confused with the facts.

"Say, Shawna, you like Terence or what?"

She blushes at that, says, "Let's just get on the phone right now, mister."

Well, I'm down from sir to mister but still stuck. She heads for the phone, gets all her eighth-grade girlfriends lined up for next Saturday, then tells me to do the same. I say I have to get phone numbers from Terence, but she only frowns at that and calls Mrs. Bidden at the rectory. Gets all those names and numbers, then actually sits with me while I make the calls. Most of them say they're in, and it is left to me to collect the stuff we'll need and line up a filling station. I don't call Terence, though. I'm wondering if he's figured out those are Rufus's tracks. He has to know, as we'd left in such a hurry that his room was a complete mess. What burglars would only look in a kid's room and leave all that gear of his dad's?

I don't know, he might be planning his own brand of beating. What I do know is that Billy and I had better step lightly for a while.

CHAPTER 23

GEORGIE GETS TO SEE BUSTER, AND BILLY AND I
get more rags than we can use. Buster doesn't
act like she knows us at all. She has a pen made out
of pitchforks and tractor wheels and old rusted saws
and a hundred kinds of tools stuck in the ground.
Mr. Laughlin could have been an artist if he wasn't a
junk man. All that stuff is hammered into the earth
at just the right angle to make a nice pen and look
good, too. Buster has fresh straw in there and a little
half shed to keep the sun off her should she like.
Even Georgie understands Buster has it better where
she is now than she did with us.

We go over and borrow some buckets from Mrs. Kanagaki, and I thank her proper for those tools she'd given me. She is pleased about it, I can tell, says I can come around and fix little things for her from time to time and that we can have another chat. Grandpa gets us the soap from the grocery. A five-pound box of it. All you have to do is mix it with water and you'll have more suds than you need, he tells us. Betsy and Shawna and the twins make some signs. SAN JOAQUIN BOYS CAR WASH. TWENTY-FIVE CENTS DONATION.— Even, STOP—drawn like a real stop sign, which is a bit pushy, if you ask me. No one does.

All we have to do is get a gas station to let us use their water and their spot. There are five filling stations in Orange Grove City, unless you count the truck stop out on the highway. We want Russ Mueller's station as it's on a nice shady block right in the middle of a regular neighborhood with lots of the kind of traffic that goes by lazy. It's a street with a center strip that's got big redwood trees they decorate up with Christmas lights every December and just the thing, we think. Folks around there are the well-heeled ones.

Russ is inside his little metal-and-glass house with the door shut and his cooler on when we drop by.

We knock and go in, polite, the little bell over the doorjamb tinkling.

"Mr. Mueller, how are you doing today?" I say.

"Air's out where it always is, kids. No charge for filling your tires," Russ says. He's a redheaded German with red eyelashes and red hairs sprouting from his ears, but no red on his head, as he's gone bald early. "Thanks, Mr. Mueller," I say. "We don't have any tires need air."

He nods and goes back to reading the racing form he has on his little metal table there.

"I notice you have the best filling station in Orange Grove," I say.

He looks up with one eye and nods faintly.

"Some say Richie's Shell downtown is better, but they don't know a thing."

Russ flattens his paper carefully and takes out a pencil from his shirt pocket, dabs that pencil with his tongue, and studies his paper some more.

"You know Richie charges ten cents for a five-cent soda?" I add.

"Soda machine's outside," Russ says.

Billy looks at me like, *Get on with it.*

"You got a whole lot of room on this side of the station," I say.

Russ looks up and eyes me again. "Do I know you?"

"Why, sure you do, Mr. Mueller. I'm Paolo O'Neil." I give him my best smile, all polished up like an apple special for him.

"Heard that name before."

I don't know if this is a good thing or not, so I figure the best thing is to talk fast. "Why, lots of folks know me, Mr. Mueller. I'm all around every-place all the time. I'm one of the San Joaquin altar boys." I figure that gets us closer to our topic and lets him know my reputation is foursquare.

"You go to John Muir Junior High School, though, don't you?" Russ says.

"Yes, sir."

"Hear your name around my house quite a bit." Russ blinks those red-head eyelashes, and I get it. He's Theresa Mueller's dad!

Georgie has been fiddling with the little metal Standard Oil trucks they give for ten fill-ups but looks straight at Russ and comes to his version of a rescue: "We're having a car wash here this Saturday."

Russ pushes his chair back and stands up and looks down at Georgie with his eyebrows raised. "A what?" he sniffs.

"Car wash. We got to get some money for Early Johnson's mother," Georgie says confidentially.

Russ straightens up tall and says, "You don't say?" Puts his hands on his hips and leans down to Georgie. "And what exactly is a car wash?"

"We wash people's cars for twenty-five cents. Everyone that comes in to get some gas can have one if they want."

"That's the craziest thing I heard in a long, long time, boys," he says slowly while pulling himself back upright.

I say, "It's different, but that ain't the same as crazy."

"Pretty close," he says, but he's thinking. Munching his lips and thinking. Finally, he chuckles. Shakes his head. "When is this thing supposed to happen?"

"Saturday morning, nine o'clock sharp," Georgie says happily. "You don't want to be late, Russ."

"No, wouldn't do to be late," he says to Georgie, real serious. He picks out one of those die-cast metal trucks and puts it in Georgie's hand. "You better take this. I got one more than I need." He stresses the *one,* looking at Billy and me. Then to me he says, "I got a feeling Theresa is going to get a phone call from a certain person real soon."

"Yes, sir," I say like a man about to be shot.

CHAPTER 24

Now, as I have been shot in the hand with a BB gun without no more than a little blood welt forming, dunked in the bathtub for as long as one minute, forty-five seconds without drowning, lashed to a tetherball pole for a day without dying of sunstroke, lassoed and dragged around the block with no more than my jeans getting shredded, had a tarantula tied with kite string to my wrist while I slept and never got bit—just scared well past alive when I woke up and saw it in the morning, so much so that I climbed out of the upstairs window crying like a cat that's needing love till the fire department came around to tell me I could hush up and climb back in and untie that thing from myself and could have done so without the help of the city—all that and a half dozen other experiments tried on me by Ernie for the benefit of science, I realize I have enough ideas on how to get Terence to talk. My problem is wondering whether I can, in good conscience, keep that money or not when I get it. And I am determined to get it.

I climb the stairs up to Uncle Charlie's attic room on Wednesday afternoon. Knock gentle. Wait and knock again. Wait some more. Finally open the door and peek in. Uncle Charlie is lying on his bed reading *True Detective* magazine, one of my sisters' cats asleep next to him.

"Come in," he says, and then coughs. Sounds like a leather bag full of marbles jiggling, and once he starts hacking, it takes him five minutes to stop. I wait for him to finish up, fidgeting some. I shut the door. Get a chair that's in the corner and move it close to his bed. He winds down and shakes his head. "Gets ever worse all the time," he says, giving it one more hack, swallowing hard, and looking at me. Smiles but doesn't say anything else.

I sit there for a bit, looking around. He's got a

brass statue of a horse on his dresser. A photograph of my grandfolks on my dad's side. Both of them passed before I was born. There's one picture of a pretty, dark-headed Irish girl in what I think is a genuine silver frame sitting all by itself, apart from those others.

"Uncle Charlie," I say finally, as there is nothing else to look at except his bed and the little window he's got with the shade down, "suppose you found a treasure. Couldn't you keep it?"

He doesn't say anything.

"I mean, say you know who it belongs to and they probably need it?"

Uncle Charlie blinks twice.

"It's lost. But you find it fair and square. And, for instance, when you find it, nobody has it, isn't nobody's property in particular, then. Well, maybe somebody has it, but it isn't theirs. It would be yours, wouldn't it?"

Uncle Charlie reaches for his pack of Camels, shakes one loose, and puts it between the two yellowed fingers of his right hand. Puts the cigarette in his lips and lets it dangle without lighting it.

"That'd be fair and square, I think," I say.

He scratches a kitchen match on the edge of his

nightstand and lights up, pulling that poison into himself, letting it wander out of his mouth slowly. He relaxes even more than he is already, which is a lot. The cat stands up, stretches, and dives off the bed.

"I know them that lost it need it, and I guess that gives them some claim, but it just doesn't seem fair."

Uncle Charlie puts one arm behind his head on the pillow and looks at the ceiling.

"How in the heck is a guy supposed to be somebody in this world without any money? The only ones I see get any respect are them that have it." I'm looking at his old yellow blankets.

Uncle Charlie looks like he's going to speak but changes his mind.

So I go on. "I know a fellow has more money than he knows what to do with, and he doesn't even have one actual friend. Ain't that something? Just being around him makes me feel empty sometimes." All of a sudden, I feel like I'm about to cry, and I don't know why. Uncle Charlie is still looking at the ceiling, but he puts out one hand and pats me on the knee. That's all. We just sit there together for a few minutes, and I leave. Most would never think it, but Uncle Charlie is the wisest man I've ever known in my whole life, except me.

CHAPTER 25

TERENCE IS ON HIS BEST BEHAVIOR, AS SHAWNA is there sitting at a card table with a metal tackle box for taking the quarters. I never told him about the car wash, so it's a surprise that he showed up. He hasn't got a genuine friend, but who knows how many kids he pesters. Terence is still something of a mystery to me, yet I can see well enough that he has ways of knowing the things he does. Theresa Mueller is there, thinking she's been invited as my special date because I'd phoned her, and she insists the whole time on being my shadow, running to get whatever she thinks I might need, rags or whatnot. I don't like her, but I don't not like her, either, I guess. Her dad keeps an eye out for her the whole time in between filling up cars with gas and washing his customers' windows. Arnie and Carl and Rodney, those boys from altar-boy lessons, are there and all of Shawna's girlfriends, too. And Billy.

Georgie and Rufus stand at the curb with that phony stop sign. They're happy. Fact is, we're all having a good time. That soap of my grandpa's must be some kind of special strength stuff as it makes so many suds, there are bubbles floating all down the block, and all of us are soaped up and wet too, and we haven't even had one customer yet. Mostly we are horsing around throwing soapy rags and squirting one another with the hose. When Rodney Paul squirts Vickie DeFendis and gets her shirt totally wet, Mr. Mueller steps over and shuts off the hose. Only Shawna is acting all business. Terence is hanging around her table and telling her stuff, and she's laughing little, pretty, girly laughs until he's so swelled up holding his belly in and his chest out, I think he's going to faint.

Finally, my grandpa pulls in in his Buick. He gets gas and drives around to where we are and stops and says out the window, "I need-a this automobile have-a wash, right-a now." Theresa holds the door open and leads him by the arm over to a folding chair we got there and sits him down, and we go to work. We put one pound of that five pounds of his soap on the car and scrub and hose it and dry it up in no time. He gives Shawna a quarter and drives away honking his horn all the way down the block.

Mr. Mueller has plenty of customers, and they ask all sorts of questions, curious about what we're doing, but they are all no-thank-you-and-have-fun once they get the general idea. After a couple of hours we are all sitting down on the blacktop in the shade. Mr. Mueller says we can each have a soda. As there are nine of us, it's pretty generous of him. We open the box lid and put our arms into the ice water and fish out a Nesbitt's orange or a Dr Pepper or a root beer, whichever we want. Arnie and Carl do some arm wrestling on that card table, showing off for the girls. Arnie is five foot nine or so, has a shock of corn-silk hair that's parted down the middle, and an arm like the Jolly Green Giant, and he about snaps Rodney's arm like a twig. Rodney's short like me, though dark-complexioned, with big bird eyes—as sharp-nosed as a parrot too. But he laughs easy all the time. He doesn't have that whiskey with him today. Like he did at the dance.

Terence decides he better do his bit on Shawna's account and surprises us all by beating Arnie. Takes a full minute or more, both of them going back and forth, but that Terence isn't just fat, he's got muscle under that chub. Gives me something to think about.

Finally, a middle-aged man drives up in a new '51 Nash and decides a car wash is just what he'd like. He's dressed pretty flashy with a red and blue tie and a white shirt pressed sharp. He looks over the whole scene, says he runs an automobile dealership over in Fresno. Thinks it's an interesting idea having a car wash. He says maybe we are a little before our time; shakes his head, though, and says, "But maybe only just a little."

We get on his Nash in a hurry, and this time Terence helps too. He works his way over to me and steps on my foot hard, pins me there, says, "I'll be around to see you, Paolo." I act dumb, but I get his drift. I don't know if he knows that he's under our suspicions about the money, that that's what we were after, there in his bedroom. But he's got to know it was Rufus and Billy and me laying down all those tracks on the inside of his house.

Well, I got my own plans about a meeting myself and figure sooner is just as good as later. "Come on over tomorrow," I say, wincing back pain. "We can horse around my house for a change." I'm still playing possum.

We all stay till six o'clock, when Mr. Mueller closes up, except for Rufus and Georgie, who left at noon. I'm proud of all those that helped, even though our plan is a bust. We make only fifty cents, which we give to Theresa's dad for the sodas, even though that is five cents over what they cost. He won't take it, so we give it to Theresa to put in the register on the sly. It's Carl that makes the day, though. He remembers his grandmother has a pretty good Victrola radio in her garage that he's sure we can have for Early's mom. We should have thought of a radio in the first place, as there are all kinds of shows on the radio, good stories and such and more music than you could ever own with just records.

All those guys shake my hand, Terence trying to mash it crippled for life. The girls give me hugs, and Shawna beams. Terence has the nerve to walk her home, carrying the card table, but it doesn't bother me that much. Billy and I walk along carrying our washing gear a little ways behind. We know Terence P. Gaston the Third is going to get his.

CHAPTER 26

By THE OLD YARD-SALE CLOCK IN OUR GARAGE, it's exactly eight o'clock in the morning when Terence skids in, all winded, stomach bouncing. Chasing Georgie all the way here does it to him. Georgie has called him a skunk and a badger and a possum and every varmint he knows. Has done it on our instructions.

This morning before it was light, I dragged the shoelaces of my tennis shoes across Georgie's face very gently until he woke up in a terror. Billy was ready for that and clamped his hand quick over Georgie's mouth. "Georgie," I whispered, "you got to fetch Terence for us."

Georgie was just bug eyes and confusion.

"You know how Terence doesn't like to get up till most of the day's over?"

More bug eyes and confusion.

"Well, we want to talk to Terence here right after Mom's done getting breakfast and is settled in with her sewing."

Georgie's eyes narrowed down some. Billy lifted his hand away carefully. "Why don't you go talk to Terence yourself?" Georgie asked.

"'Cause we prefer to talk to him at our house, if you have to know."

"How am I supposed to get Terence awake and over here so early?"

"Just do that hollering like you did when Billy and I were over there inside his house."

"Hollering's going to wake him; how's it going to get him to come over here?"

"You are going to call him names."

"I am?" Georgie's eyes rolled up in his head just a little as he imagined that. Then he smiled. I do believe it's true that thinking positive is good for you, and there was Georgie making an attitude change right there, another example.

I nodded down at him with approval.

"What names you think I ought to call him?" Georgie was thinking hard then but enjoying the work.

That's when I told him the varmint names and such. He wanted to add swamp turtle and water snake because of a picture book he'd been reading of late, but I told him we'd stick to field animals for today.

Anyway, here is Terence now, riled up, fierce. If you ever corner one of those rat creatures, you'll know exactly what I mean. They ain't big like Terence, but they will chew an arm off you if you get too close and they'll enjoy it. Naturally, Georgie comes to hide behind me and Billy in that garage.

Billy and I don't pay any attention to Terence at all. I'm busy cinching Billy into an old life vest. Terence is blinking in that brown light and wiping his nose. And I say, cool as a breeze, "Hey, Terence, give me a hand with this thing."

"What for?" Terence says, gruff and still huffing.

Billy points to the rafters. There is an old double block and tackle fitted to the main beam my dad rigged to pull an old engine once. We attached a line through the pulleys to the life vest, and I am just finishing strapping it firmly to Billy.

"What are you trying to do?" says Terence, genuinely curious enough to forget Georgie for a minute but still acting tough and unfriendly, knowing we still have business undone.

"Whatta you think I'm going to do? I'm going to pull him up high so he can look around like Errol Flynn or somebody in the movies," I say, like he's completely ignorant.

"Why don't you just climb up on top of the garage if you want to look around?" Terence asks, all suspicious.

I stop my tying. "There. That'll hold him." Then I turn my attention to Terence. "'Cause there ain't no sport in that. Now, c'mon, help me hoist him."

Billy looks kind of funny, like a lacquered wooden doll with a smile painted on its face. I grab the rope and hand some to Terence. We both begin to pull. Billy's toes lift off the dirt floor as the old pulleys squeak. He looks stiffer and more uncomfortable than ever, but he keeps smiling like he's having the time of his life. We get him all the way up and are hanging on to that rope and grunting. Terence and I tire of holding Billy's weight pretty quick, even with some of it being subtracted by those pulleys, so we let him down.

Billy smiles large and gives us the okay sign, nodding his head. *Yes, yes!*

Terence squints at us, then at the rafters, and he says, slowly, "Okay, my turn."

Very matter-of-fact, I say, "Terence, I'd like to, but you're too heavy. And besides, my dad wouldn't like it."

"I'm not too heavy, and your father isn't home. You can just pull me up and let me right back down."

Billy signs to me, and I say out loud to Terence what is his meaning: *Maybe you should let him. He helped you pull me up.*

"Is all that . . . that stuff really necessary?" Terence can't get that snob out of himself. "You do realize, don't you, that there is no way they'll ever let him be an altar boy." He's looking at Billy and says hard, "But the little stinker is right. I did help pull him up."

Billy and I start tying him in quick. A little too quick, maybe, but Terence looks pleased enough, waiting on his ride. We haul on that rope with everything we got and finally get him up. Terence is saying the vest is too tight and he wants to come down and fix it. We tie the rope off to a hook in one of the garage studs and step back, and Georgie and me start chuckling. Terence is hollering and kicking and swearing. I got to admit he looks pretty foolish up there. We're feeling fine. Not Billy. Billy is a gentle one, but he's sensitive about his signing as it's still new, and I think he feels as if Terence tried to smash a new toy of his.

Then something happens I don't quite expect. Billy picks up the bamboo pole we have there to jab Terence with till he tells us all we want to know. But Billy whacks him one good on the knees instead. Then he hits him again in the stomach. Terence starts hollering. Billy's got his eyes half closed and his mouth set hard in an even line. Like he doesn't see anyone else in that garage but Terence and maybe not even him. I think maybe he's seeing all them that left him out of things his whole life.

Well, he hits Terence again. On the tip of his elbow. The crack of the bamboo echoes sharp off the walls, and Terence quits hollering and starts to crying. He's scared now. His eyes keep swiveling to see where Billy is going to hit him next and trying to see how he can get out of there and knowing he isn't going to get out of there.

Billy stops and hands me that bamboo pole. He signs, quick, *You got to hit him too.*

Georgie runs out of the garage.

I know I feel sorry for Terence now. But I know Billy is right. I can't leave him to do a job I got started. So I hit Terence, hard. He looks at me funny, like he's confused as to where he is, and then blood pops out from his ear as if it has been waiting its whole life to get out and is happy to escape and run down his neck like it ain't his blood at all, only on loan, with no loyalty to him whatsoever.

I say, "Where is that money, Terence?" I feel I am about to throw up, but I say it.

Terence looks at me as if he understands for the first time why he's hanging there. He says right off, "It's in the hold of that schooner. I rolled it up and slipped it in there." He's breathing roughly. "I don't care about it. Just let me down. Please. Paolo? Please."

I'm in some kind of shock. Billy gets an ax from the back of the garage and chops that rope where it's tied, and Terence drops down like a sack of potatoes and just lies there. Billy leans over him holding that ax, and I have the presence of mind to warn Terence that if he tells anyone of what has gone on here, we will chop his ears off. He's just moaning and whimpering. We look him over carefully and see he ain't actually hurt bad, only scared to his spine—and now just relieved. Confessing is good for you. But I don't feel good. Billy has calmed down, and whatever demon fired up in him and started its burning has been snuffed like a candle thumbed out in the darkness, and we're just, both of us, standing there, spent.

CHAPTER 27

TERENCE FINISHES UP HIS WHIMPERING AFTER A bit, which is good because we still have a few questions. At least, I have some. Billy is sitting on my toolbox in the corner with his arms crossed, looking foul. Terence is still sitting on the dirt floor of the garage when I ask him, "So exactly how did you find the money?"

He tells me that he found the little canvas bag of collection money on a chair up on the altar after practice on a Monday and buried it in the Monsignor's garden after everybody left. Came back the next day on his Bianchi racer without his dad to get it. "Why didn't you spend it, Terence?" I ask.

"I had other plans for it," he says quietly. Won't say what those plans were, as he can tell we are done being questioners or else he just doesn't care. You take all a fellow's got like we took Terence's pride, and he's got nothing to lose then and won't care what you do to him after that and will just please himself. He's right, acting like that. And I know now that raising a stick to anybody is a bad idea, as that stick has a life of its own, and there is no saying when you can put it back down.

Those two look something terrible, so I say we should get on and go out of that garage and walk some in the orchards, then go get the money. Billy glances at me, wondering what I'm up to, I guess, but I'm thinking just what I've said. It's ugly in that garage. I walk Terence, gentle like, down a hard-packed dirt lane that runs off from our place and into the orchards. Billy is riding that racer very slowly next to us. Terence is walking along, kind of inside of himself, so I drop back just a bit and sign to Billy, *Money. We keep. Yes?*

Billy looks at me like he's made out of wood or stone, his eyes looking somewhere just past my left ear.

I don't know all the signs for what I want to say, and Terence is too close and would hear me if I talked, so I make like I'm digging, then wiping sweat off my face, and then like I'm swinging that bamboo pole and so on. My idea is, we already done all the work of locating the money, so maybe we should keep it.

Billy keeps on with his statue-staring at me.

Terence turns around and says, "I don't care what you do with the money."

My ears bloom up red, and Billy makes the littlest of smiles.

But we don't go directly to Terence's place. We spend the day half moping, half horsing around, mostly sitting in a giant fig tree, sucking the sweet insides out of those that we picked and just watching things: birds and bugs and the sky. It's like we don't want to go get the money, 'cause then what will we do? Least ways, that's how it was for me. I think Terence just likes being outside, letting the sky and the sun wash him down with their comfort.

We do go on to Terence's place eventually, though, and that money is right there where he said it was. We snap off the bottom of that ship, and there is the roll of bills. Seventy-nine dollars exactly.

Terence tossed the loose change. Billy signs he wants to hold it, and I give it to him. He seems to weigh it, likes the feel of it, I can tell.

As it's five thirty in the afternoon and time for us to go home, I say so and take back the cash and just stuff it in my pocket. Billy doesn't even give me a look. We are heading out through the kitchen when the phone rings. Terence, for probably the first time in his life, doesn't seem interested in picking it up. So I do.

It's Shawna. Says she knows Georgie didn't go with us as he'd been in the house crying a little but wouldn't say why. Now he's missing, and she's in a panic. I sort of understand what she's saying, as dinner is at five at our house and Georgie's never missed it his whole six years unless he's been with us. "And Rufus, he's nowhere to be found either," she cries.

And I know then that it's serious.

CHAPTER 28

Grandpa and Hector and my mother and all the girls are there when Billy and Terence and I race up on Terence's bikes. Ernie's digging line somewhere out in the desert for PG&E this week, and Dad's somewhere between Kansas and Colorado on his way home as usual. Right on our tails, though, come Arnie, Rodney, and Carl on their bikes. I suppose Shawna called them, too. Anyhow, I am glad of them.

Grandpa is too upset and is jabbering in Italian back and forth with my mom, so it's Hector that lays out a plan. Grandpa will drive around in his Buick.

The twins will go with him as spotters, as they have eyes younger than his. Hector is going out through the vineyard that borders the back of our place and will take Shawna and Margarita and Betsy and Carl with him. I am supposed to go with the rest of the guys out the other way through the fig orchards that fan out from the other side of our place. I feel so guilty, I can't think to tell those boys what to do. I know it's what Georgie saw in the garage that upset him and set him to wandering with Rufus, who probably seemed to Georgie the only one he could count on just then.

It's Terence that gives the orders. It's like he's the old Terence who ordered us around at his house, except now it's different. He's not trying to boss, just trying to help. He knows this is for real and so do I. Shawna breaks loose of her group and comes back to us and is standing next to him. He seems taller somehow then, with her there. We will each take a row and leave three rows between ourselves and the next guy. We'll just walk till we hit Brawley Avenue, which marks the end of that grove of figs, and then figure what to do after that. It seems as good a plan as any to me. Rodney is an excitable one and runs down his row. Arnie stomps along, powdery dust billowing up from his boot steps, his eyes on the ground as if he's tracking. Shawna walks the same row as Terence. Billy is on his own three rows over from me.

Suddenly, we see Billy is jumping and grunting, and he goes running, a little dust devil zigzagging behind him before it winds down and collapses. He comes back with Rufus by the collar, and Rufus is wet! We gather around, and I know it's bad because Rufus is scared of water and never goes in. He must have been dragged in or fell in, or I just don't know. The only place to fall in any water is the ditch or a rancher's livestock pond. There's no livestock around here until you get up to the foothills, excepting for dairies, and there are none of those on this side of Orange Grove City.

I say all that, and the others know it already, excepting the part about Rufus being afraid of water. Arnie says, "Let's follow Rufus's wet tracks." And so we do without hesitating any, trampling along over one another in our hurry and fear. It's already well after six o'clock, and the air is getting specked with bits of dark. Sun is a plum spoiling on an old tablecloth of clouds. Doves twinkling in for cover and water, wings catching the last of the light. Everything in nature so soft and pretty, yet I see now, always full of hard danger.

We run a couple of hundred yards, and there is the ditch. There are a hundred ditches around Orange Grove City, all of them with ice water, even on the hottest of days, as that water is from high in the Sierras. We come right up on the spot where Rufus's tracks end and see plain enough how the dirt is caved in, where Georgie must have slipped and pulled Rufus in with him, and where Rufus climbed back out.

It's still light enough that we can see up and down that canal. It's one of the small ones that cuts off a main one bringing water to this particular ranch. But it is deeper than it looks, we all know, and cold enough to make your arms too numb to move. That's why we always just float down a bit from one bridge to the next on our tubes. We climb out on those metal ladders they set every so often into the concrete of the bridges. Georgie isn't likely to have a tube, just going for a lonesome walk like I suspect he was doing.

Terence tells Arnie and Rodney to run down one way and the rest of us will go the other. So we go down another hundred yards or so, where that little ditch cuts a quick dogleg west. And just around that bend is Georgie, stuck like a leaf to the metal grating below the little concrete bridge.

He looks as white as ice, and his mouth and nose are just above the waterline. He hasn't planned it that way. He's just stuck by the cold and the current in that one exact position and couldn't move an inch no matter how hard he were to try. His eyes are egg yolks, and he's too scared to cry or yell anything to us.

"Oh my God, Georgie! Don't move!" Shawna shouts because she can't not shout something. She knows he can't move. We know that water can move him anytime it cares to, though. It's a bad spot. Those grates come halfway down from the tops of the bridges to catch trash. Georgie could be pulled under, easy, and there'd be no hope for him then. On the other hand, if it weren't for that grating, he'd already be drowned.

"We got to go back and get a rope!" I shout to Terence. Billy looks at Terence, waiting to see if Terence wants him to run for one.

Terence shakes his head. "You can run for help if you want, but I'd rather have your help here. There is no time to lose." He's already sitting down in the dirt, taking his tennis shoes off. He strips off his shirt, his rolls of fat showing, and then says, "Excuse me" to Shawna, who turns around, and he takes off his jeans, too. He's standing there in his underwear, and he's not a pretty one, and he's a little shamed but not much. It's Billy and I got the shame on us, as we can see he's got blue bruises all over him, a white horse we made into an Appaloosa, those horses with spots on them. He doesn't hesitate then and goes to the edge and dives in. He comes up right away and sweeps right to that grate and has his arms up to catch it and does. With his strong arms, he pulls himself up some and lets the current paste him to the grating right next to Georgie. Shawna is down on her knees in the dust, hands over her mouth. Billy and I are running to stand above them on the little bridge. But there's nothing we can do.

Then Terence pushes himself off that grate with a mighty effort and grabs Georgie and drags him under, and they disappear under the grate. In two seconds they pop up like dark pups on the other side of the bridge, and Terence is swimming, one-armed, angling toward the bank as the current sweeps them along. We run to keep up with them. Maybe two hundred yards of them rushing with the water until there is another small bridge and one of those metal ladders. And with Georgie in one of his arms, Terence grabs hold of it and climbs out, all of himself straining, all his muscles working, and he slow yet sure of himself.

He drops down in the dirt, and Georgie rolls off to his side like a little sogged dog, heavy as the dead. But he's not, and Shawna is on him, checking his breathing and rubbing his limbs and slapping his legs and chest and face. Terence sits up slowly, breath chuffing like a steam locomotive. Billy and I come up on him, and those others have come up our way too. Terence has his head down, and his shoulders start slowly to shaking, and we can see that he's crying, crying with relief, crying for everything that ever was in his life, maybe crying for his mom and crying for his dad and crying he's got no friends and is a thief. And Billy kneels down and takes Terence's head in his arms. And they both cry for the same reasons, I guess.

CHAPTER 29

TERENCE IS SOMEBODY. GETS HIS PICTURE IN the paper on Tuesday to prove it. And, you know, it is just fine with me. Shawna has him over in the evening for chocolate cake she bakes herself. They sit on our porch, only eight or nine pairs of eyes like fireflies in the dark windows behind them. The whole time she is looking at him like he's Kirk Douglas or some other movie star. All dreamy. Spoons him the cake like he's a baby. I have to stop watching. I guess I never knew that Shawna could be lonely too, not with me and Georgie and Billy around all the time to keep her with plenty of company.

Anyway, it's the first time I see her so happy. Maybe she won't have to be reading all the time and lose her vision and be an old maid, teach school, and take up drinking after all, like I expected. Maybe love ain't blind, as she saw in Terence what nobody else did.

Next day Billy and I are walking out to Early Johnson's place with Carl's grandma's Victrola radio. We stop by and ask Terence if he'll go with us. He says okay, and we go out Early's way taking turns lugging that radio. Terence doesn't talk as much as usual, gone kind of thoughtful, and it's less of a stress to be around him.

We ask Terence along for a reason, but we aren't sure how we are going to give him that reason. When we finally get out to Early's, he's not home yet. We can't decide whether to wait on him or not. We don't knock on the door, 'cause if his mother does hear us, she might not be able to get to the door, or maybe she'd be scared someone is out to do her some harm. And, too, out in the country most have shotguns, even old ladies in wicker wheelchairs, and she could easily mistake us for trouble. I can imagine ringing her bell and that door opening and both of them barrels laid over the bridge of my nose like a pair of glasses, then me only smoke and some bits of my clothes Billy could sell for souvenirs.

Billy starts showing Terence a couple of signs. Little stuff. *I have a great thirst. I feel sick in my stomach. I'm sorry.* And so on. Terence signs it all back exactly, and I say the words, slow. We all feel a bit better then; we know we're talking about what happened in that garage. We decide to leave the Victrola on the porch. Billy thinks if Early gets grateful, we might be in danger of a bear hug, and that might even set Early off further toward that warm disposition of his. We haven't got pencil or paper, so we scratch out in the dirt with a stick in deep letters that won't blow away: *Mr. Johnson, This is for your mother—from the boys of San Joaquin.*

Walking home, Billy pokes me in the side with his finger.

"Terence, here is the money," I say. I take it out of my jeans and hand it to him. I've got it rolled tight with a rubber band.

He looks at it like it's a poisonous spider.

"We can't keep it. 'Cause of the church. You do what you want with it. But . . . well, Terence—Billy and I think you should give it to Monsignor. Tell him you found it."

Terence doesn't say anything, but he takes it into his hand, holds it softly.

"You deserve to have folks at the church be glad of you. After what you did for Georgie. After we . . ."

Terence smiles a crooked, sad smile. Billy and I are watching these shadows and figures running across his face when a car comes down the road, dust rolling off its back end like barrels of brown smoke. It stops where we are, and the dust rolls past us, powdering us down. It's Jimmy and Margarita, the front end of that Plymouth all fixed. "Hey, guys," Margarita says. "What are you doing out here?"

I figure I know what they are doing out here. Those shady clumps of sycamores out past Early's place would be a good spot to watch the sun set. "We took that Victrola to Early's mom," I say. Suddenly, I feel a little brightness, more than I've felt in a lot of days, glad that my smashing up Jimmy's car didn't smash up their friendship.

"Where to, fellas?" Jimmy says.

We look at each other.

"The rectory," Terence says dully.

CHAPTER 30

MONSIGNOR PUTS THE PHONE DOWN. HE LEANS back in his leather chair, that leather squeaking. He makes a little church of his hands and points it to his lips. He looks at us sadly. "I hate to make a call like that to one of my boys' fathers." He looks at me. At Billy. I'm sick to my stomach, wanting to tell my side of things. I know I have to. But . . . I can't. Not after what Terence told me and Billy in front of the cathedral after Jimmy and Margarita dropped us off. I just roll my Dodgers cap in my hands.

We sit there, the windows already black, the wood paneling rich and dark. If I'd been in that office for any other reason, I'd be enjoying myself. We all have our own leather chairs to sit in. Monsignor has all kinds of books and statues in there for company. In fact, when we came in, he was sitting in that big chair of his with the Bible open on his lap, listening to *The Whistler* radio show on his RCA. Turned it off, though. Opened a window to let some of the smoke out. We're lucky, as it's a Wednesday and he had to stay here for confessions till six thirty and didn't go out after to Murphey's. If lucky is what we are. It seems like forever, waiting. The wooden clock standing behind Monsignor's head says seven thirty when Mrs. Bidden peeks in asking Monsignor if he'd like some warm milk or cookies or something, but really so as she can get a look at us, hungry herself for all possible gossip. He just waves her off. She goes, leaving the door open a crack.

Monsignor leans back in his chair and says, "Boys, I want to pray on this while we're waiting." He closes his eyes and falls dead asleep, little whistling sounds coming out of the tunnels of his nose. Other than that, it's so quiet, we hear that big Cadillac plainly when it squeals to a stop out front. A minute later Mrs. Bidden comes in with

Mr. Gaston, points him toward Monsignor, and leaves. Monsignor sits up with a start and looks around and then at us like, *Who are you?* Then he sees Mr. Gaston standing there, a dark cloud on his face, wearing a pair of gray slacks, a yellow golf shirt, and house slippers.

Monsignor rises and asks Mr. Gaston to sit and then sits down himself. Mr. Gaston's so nervous, he sits and then stands right back up. Monsignor's not quite awake, and he gets up again with him and then sits down again, sort of growling to himself. When he finally gets himself situated, he tells Mrs. Bidden that will be all, and the door that hasn't quite closed yet shuts sharply with an angry ghost's bang. Then Terence just starts telling it all again. How he found that money and stole it, how he buried it and dug it back up, kept it and would have gone on keeping it if I hadn't discovered it and made him turn himself in.

All through the telling, Billy is making himself as small as he can in his chair, as if he'd prefer to disappear. He's clearly relieved when the story is done and his name never comes up. Monsignor takes the money out of the drawer of his desk and unfolds it on the table. "I'm afraid it's true, Mr. Gaston. And it's all here—except about twenty-five dollars."

Mr. Gaston has been sitting there the whole time, his jaw dropping down a little bit more with each bit of the telling. He's too shocked to be mad. He's looking at Terence as if he doesn't know him, and the truth is, he doesn't, I guess. Terence looks right back at him, and then his eyes gentle and fall away. Monsignor makes a little cough, and Mr. Gaston looks over at him, dazed. "I think as Terence has returned the money and expressed his remorse, there is no reason to inform the police." Mr. Gaston hasn't got that far in his thinking. You can tell by the fact he's lost the powers of his tongue. "I was thinking, however, that Paolo might deserve a small reward for his efforts—say, ten dollars?"

Mr. Gaston nods, but just sits there.

"Of course, in a private matter like this I wouldn't know who to ask for a contribution."

It's Terence who says, "Dad, give Paolo ten dollars." And his dad fumbles immediately with his wallet, but his hands are so shaky, he can't get any one bill out. Terence takes the wallet from him and, expert, snags a ten, leans over, and hands it to me.

Monsignor is a sharp one and says to me, "I wouldn't go around crowing about your getting

Terence to come in, Paolo." I nod my head with some vigor at that.

"And, of course, there's the twenty-five that's still missing." Terence takes two more tens and a five out of the wallet and puts the money on Monsignor's desk. Monsignor nods his head in satisfaction. He slips it off the table, lickety-split, and silent as that guy at the fair, slides it into his drawer. "Now, Mr. Gaston, I was thinking there should be a rather serious punishment for this."

Mr. Gaston nods weakly.

"In fact, I've spoken to Terence about it, and he feels that he should not be let out of your sight for, perhaps, a year."

Terence snaps to attention, as no such discussion has occurred.

"If he's having dinner, then you are there making sure he eats everything put in front of him and that he washes the dishes without complaint and to your satisfaction. If you go golfing or to play tennis, well, then Terence will just have to go along."

Terence's eyes light up with what looks like admiration of Monsignor.

"It's a hard thing for a boy to have to spend all his time with an adult, but I don't see how we can let him off with anything less."

Mr. Gaston shakes himself loose from his silence and says, "Yes, well . . ."

But Monsignor cuts him off. "And I'll have Terence report to me weekly to be sure there is no shirking." He nods solemnly and finishes with, "On his part." Mr. Gaston and Monsignor lock eyes, and a little eye-wrestling match goes on for about five seconds, just long enough for Terence to shoot me a grin of wonder. And then it is over.

We leave the office together, and Mr. Gaston asks us, distractedly, if we want a ride. We say we feel like a walk in the night air, and so Terence the Second and Terence the Third get in their big, white Cadillac and drive slowly away.

Walking home under the black trees, there's a fast dark sky running white clouds high overhead, and Billy and I take our time. When we come to the last block of the city and step off into the dirt sidewalk that runs along the county road past our house, we can see all the lights on at home. It looks like a ship that's having a party on board. And I'm glad our captain will be home in a couple of days. "Billy," I say, "do you really think Terence would have never spoken to Shawna again if we'd told how he came in on his own? If he'd have dropped her after he'd gone and stole her heart?" It was highly doubtful, I knew, on account of Terence's lonesomeness. I hadn't argued with him 'cause if he wanted to make heroes out of us, why should I have stopped him. Billy's face is hard to see in that dark, but I imagine he's smiling.

CHAPTER 31

A NEW TIRE AND WHEEL, A HANDLEBAR-MOUNTED light, and some plastic white and green ribbons to trail off the bar grips cost nine dollars and ninety-five cents. Chester's so suspicious of our having a ten, he holds it up to the light before he gives us our change. On the way home Billy and I split a Nesbitt's lime we bought with the nickel. We sit outside Russ Mueller's place to drink it. Russ comes out and asks if we mind moving out of the way so his customers can pull in. I tell him he doesn't have to worry as we have an eye out for them and can move when they come. He says something like, "Oh, so that's how it is" and asks if he should give Theresa a call then for me as I'm going to be hanging around and she could be down to the station on her bike in five minutes. I tell him thanks, but it so happens that we have to hurry home. Which is true, anyhow, as my dad came home yesterday, and Monsignor and a whole slew of folks are coming to dinner. I've decided Theresa is a good kid, just not old enough for boys yet.

Last night, going up to bed, I saw Billy and Dad having a signing conversation. Billy's hands were fluttering quick as birds, and my dad was doing a lot of nodding and a little signing, too. There's plenty of my dad to go around, and I didn't mind.

We get home and put Billy's bike up in the garage. He locks it with a chain heavy enough to anchor the *Queen Mary,* that big ship of the queen's. We go up the back steps and are surprised to find that it's Hector and Grace from the diner making that love seat squeak. Hector looks up, and I think for a second he's got jam all over his face till I see Grace is wearing lipstick. "Hi, Little Hector," she says, her voice a quick, rough song.

"Hi," I say, and go in, smirking, Billy right behind. Monsignor is sitting at the head of the table, and Grandpa is facing him. This time Dad's in the middle with my mom. The girls are doing all the serving tonight. Grandma has Maria-Teresina-the-Little-Rose on her lap. Ernie is out on the front porch playing chess with Uncle Charlie, and the two of them won't come in. Either they're locked in mortal combat or else Ernie must want some of that Hamm's beer. Georgie is happily slipping spaghetti to Rufus under the table, which puts them both on shaky ground as grace hasn't even been said.

The doorbell rings, and Shawna freezes where she's standing, just now setting down a bowl of meat sauce. The twins go for the door and come back with Terence the Third, and Terence the Second, who's looking a little sheepish. He looks at Stony the crow and at two of the cats asleep on top of the radio, and his eyes do this miniature side to side so quick, you'd miss it if you weren't me and watching close. Shawna lights up and brings them to the table. The light isn't glowing on her face, it's burning from inside her, coming out through her skin. You could probably warm your hands just by passing them over her cheeks.

I look at Monsignor, and he's tossing back a glass of red wine, and I see it's Jimmy Assayian that's filling him another. Monsignor told me and

Billy yesterday, when we went by for confession, that our penance for questioning Terence as hard as we did and spending that five dollars at the carnival is to take our lessons together so we can serve Mass side by side, me saying the Latin and Billy pouring the water and wine.

Monsignor says the blessing, and we commence to eating, excepting Maria-Teresina-the-Little-Rose, who is both eating her spaghetti and making strange jewelry of it. Everybody's talking, and even Mr. Gaston starts in on a little halting half conversation with Margarita and my mom. I sit there for a minute in the middle of all that, and I feel good, and then it seems, for a bit, as if there's no sound, just mouths moving and plates going around. I see Terence looking up from his plate at Shawna as if she's Mother Mary and he's come fifty miles on his knees to see her, and Shawna is blinking, sort of petting his weariness down with her eyelashes. And I see how sometimes things work the way they're supposed to without my meddling or care.

I get this tingly feeling all through my body—up my neck and over my scalp, down my arms and out even to the very tips of my fingers. And I look at my hands and know, right then, that I must be somebody, 'cause this has to be what a body feels like when it's truly alive.

Then all the noise of the clinking and clattering and laughing comes back, comes swooshing in like the tide rolling up and filling holes in the sand, except it's my ears that fill with the sounds, and I glance up to see Alice-Ann and Aurora bugging their eyes at their hands held in front of them, like I must have just then seemed to them to have been doing, them being their best little brides of Frankenstein for me, just so I'll know I'm not dreaming, that I'm just home, just Paolo, and real.

ACKNOWLEDGMENTS

I would like to express my appreciation to
Barbara Markowitz, my agent,
and to Richard Jackson, editor, teacher.